The Amazon Chronicles

SARAH MÄKELÄ

Copyright © 2013 Sarah Mäkelä

Published by Kissa Press LLC

Editor: Katriena Knights
Cover Artist: The Killion Group

ISBN: 0991046900
ISBN-13: 978-0-9910469-0-4

DEDICATION

To my wonderful husband, my supportive mom, and my amazing cats who
provided plenty of inspiration for the werecats.

CONTENTS

ACKNOWLEDGMENTS

Special thanks to Kinley Baker for loving *Jungle Heat* and believing in it.
Thanks to everyone at Changeling Press who first published these novellas.
I'd almost given up hope that I'd find a publisher. Also to Kim Killion for
her amazing work on the cover.

JUNGLE HEAT

1

Adara raced over the dense forest floor, trying to escape the shadow closing on her heels. Fear pumped adrenaline through her body as she ran toward her village through the darkness. Panic tangled with the sheer need to survive. *If only I'd listened. What was I thinking, coming out alone?*

She shot a glance over her shoulder. Her foot smacked against a tree root in the moment of distraction, pitching her body forward. The fall came in slow motion.

Cursing under her breath, she rolled onto her back. Dry leaves clung to her blonde hair. The subtle, musty scent of slow rot rose from the rich soil, mixed with the predator's distinct smell. The dark shadow loomed. Her gaze rose to take in her pursuer, wondering if the beast would be her doom.

The tall, broad-shouldered creature towered over her. Watching. It wasn't human or animal. The village Wise Woman had warned her of beings like this, but they'd seemed like fables. How could something so fantastical be real?

Even as she trembled with fear, this creature captivated her. The black and orange stripes covering his shoulders and arms evoked a distant memory, yet the design was uncommon in the Amazon.

His hair hung in straight, black strands like a human's, but his face had the nose, mouth, and eyes of a feline. His muscular, naked body reflected a splendid combination of both species. Sweat-shiny skin glistened through the inch-long fur that covered him.

His white chest intrigued her, all the way to the patch of fur barely covering his groin.

Leaves and branches framed his face with a lush green background. He crouched over her. His piercing golden eyes focused solely on her. His stare reminded her of a cat from her village staring at a small rodent before pouncing.

As he leaned down, she grabbed her kris from the garter on her thigh and pushed it against his stomach. She didn't want today to be the day she died. Her people needed her. She wouldn't let this beast deny them their princess.

The animal cocked his head at her. He brushed his lips over her throat, whiskers tickling her chin.

Her body stiffened. *What is he doing?* Bewilderment spread through her as his feline lips touched her neck. Instead of biting her, his canines grazed lightly, gently, from just below her ear down to her shoulder, almost as if exploring her flesh, instead of seeking to rip open her throat.

She tensed. Even with her weapon pressed against the beast's stomach, she still feared for her life. As an Amazon princess, she wasn't easily scared. But this feline made her heart pound. If only she had brought Rubia with her. She wouldn't be in this situation and could've stood a better chance against this feline.

Why does he persist in toying with me? Adara swallowed as a low burn started in the pit of her stomach. These feelings confused her.

A soft sniffing sounded in her ear right before his tongue scraped rough caresses on her skin. Other jungle cats marked their territory. Did this animal believe she was his? She didn't want to find out.

Without waiting for the feline's next move, Adara drove the kris deep into his stomach, meeting resistance as it plunged through flesh and muscle. She forced it further as his blood flowed onto her hands, making the hilt of the kris slick, weakening her grip.

He roared and leapt back with her kris still embedded in his abdomen.

She scrambled to her feet. His scream so near the side of her face made her ear ring. Bringing up a hand to her ear, Adara felt a trail of his wet blood drip along her cheek.

He straightened his spine and strode back to her, her kris still buried in him as if it were nothing more than a minor annoyance to him. She clenched her hands into fists and dropped them to her sides.

The reality of what she saw struck her. She froze. How could he act so unaffected? He shouldn't have been able to move around so casually. It wasn't possible. *How can I outrun something like that? This can't be happening.*

Her mother had always warned her to be careful when traveling through the forest. Why hadn't she listened? And how could she feel so drawn to this animal when he intimidated her?

"Who are you?" Gritting her teeth, she forced her voice to resonate with the commanding tones of an Amazon huntress, and fervently hoped it didn't betray the panic racing through her veins. Her people's beliefs restricted them from showing fear in front of strangers. Not that they saw many. But her tribeswomen were survivors in dangerous times. Their history brimmed with reminders.

The feline bared pointed white teeth. "Call me Rei." His husky voice reverberated like a deep growl.

He launched into the air and, before she could react, flattened her to the ground. Air whooshed out of her lungs. Her eyes widened and locked onto his.

He pinned her arms next to her head and pressed his feline lips to hers. His tongue scraped across her lower lip, causing nips of pain to cut through the alluring sensation.

She shook her head hard, breaking the kiss. Her breath rushed out short and quick. Never before had she kissed anyone. His mouth on hers created fiery stirrings within her body that felt almost too good. Her racing pulse only spread the warmth throughout her body that much faster.

Twice a year, her tribeswomen associated with Indian men. The younger girls were forced to stay in a hut during those visits, although Adara had snuck out once with Rubia in a fit of rebellion. She'd spotted one of her kin pressing her mouth against an Indian male's. *Could this be what happens?*

But men weren't to be trusted. Her kin had learned that the hard way many, many years ago.

Her mind flashed to the tales she'd heard from the Wise Woman. Horrible reminders assaulted her, memories of the men from long ago, enslaving her kind, killing them ruthlessly with diseases and swords.

She could imagine the cruelty of the conquering, pillaging men as vividly as if she had been there herself, so strongly had the Wise Woman spoken. It had taken weeks for her to sleep soundly after listening to that story.

Sudden alarm swept away the lust that burned inside her. This creature could do the same. *He's chased me, after all.*

"What do you want from me?" Adara asked, trying to sound strong, but instead her voice came out husky. She cleared her throat and returned his gaze.

Talking with an animal! Rubia would be jealous. Her tribeswomen would never believe this story... if she survived the encounter.

Rei smiled, warmth emanating from him. "You." His chest rumbled, and he rolled the word off his tongue like an exotic purr.

Raising an eyebrow, she scrunched up her face. "Me?" Her voice croaked, and she hastily cleared her throat again. "Why?"

She hadn't expected to hear that word. Besides, he didn't fit into the category of people who wanted her. Only her village would not last without the protection and guidance she offered it.

"I've watched you for a while now. Your strength and sincerity make you magnificent." He caressed her cheek, the roughness of his fingertips abrasive against her skin, and the sharp claws at their ends never far from her thoughts.

"You've been watching me?" A frown tugged at her lips, wariness settling in where the lust once caressed. "Why did you chase me?" Her words cut through the humid night air like a blade.

"Because you ran. Sometimes, I love a game of cat and mouse." He smirked, distorting his catlike face. Pain darkened his features, and he gripped the hilt of her kris, pulling it out of his stomach. His ripped flesh had already started to heal around the blade.

The kris dripped with crimson blood as he handed it back to her, hilt first. His palms were smeared with his own blood.

A quick glance at the wound she'd inflicted showed scarlet drops marring the crisp white fur, leaving only a thick scar where she'd shoved her blade.

"Nice sword you have there." He looked at it as if it were the first time he'd seen it. Maybe it was.

"Thanks," Adara said, trembling with trepidation and wonder. Without thinking about it, she wiped the blade in the grass, leaving dark, wet streaks of blood.

Did he pose a threat to her? She sighed. Not like her kris would do much good if he did. Besides, he hadn't rammed her through with it while he had a chance. She slid the kris back in its sheath, delicately decorated with tribal designs to grant luck and safekeeping.

She still couldn't believe the rate at which he healed. Her heart raced, but she tried to remain calm enough to think clearly. Maybe she should view this as a lesson she needed to pass so she could become an even greater queen for her people.

Glancing into his eyes, she wondered aloud, "How long have you been watching me?"

"Six months." Rei leaned his massive frame against the huge trunk of a tree. His body looked relaxed, but tension bunched in his muscles, as if he were ready to pounce if she made the wrong move. His voice sounded strange. His feline lips curved over the words in a throaty, but carefully enunciated purr that reverberated through the moist air.

Adara frowned. "How? You're not from my rainforest."

"My family originated in Russia. Siberia, to be exact. After my family escaped, I stayed in the United States and began my studies in biology. Partially to understand my people, and how life in general works. My fascination for the rainforest grew until I finally came here to conduct field research." He paused and his eyes flicked downward, as if remembering something. His gaze rose again to meet hers with his cat-like eyes. "I doubt you would recall our first meeting."

When she raised an eyebrow at him, he continued. "I had just arrived in the rainforest, set up my camp and gear, and decided to find a group of animals to observe. As a biologist on my first field assignment, I was eager

4

to get started. Then I saw a human figure walking through the forest. That struck me as odd, so I went to check it out. There you were." He huffed out a sigh. "You fascinated me so much. I didn't see the jaguar. When I heard your scream, I shifted into my tiger form to fight the cat and ensure your safety. After the battle, I couldn't figure out where you were. I wanted to make sure you were okay, so I tracked your scent to see where you had gone. Your village."

The memory washed over her. That jaguar *had* startled her. She hadn't yet gained the confidence to defend herself with her own blade then. But the foreign cat had come to her aid. There had been something too intelligent, something almost *human* in the cat's eyes.

Now she knew where she'd seen these black and orange stripes before. He had been that tiger, but also a man. She had fled as the two animals fought, never knowing what happened to either creature and never thinking about the ensuing battle, the tearing of fur, the ripping of skin with claws. The forest had been eerily silent that day when the two predators met.

"You killed the jaguar?" she asked, her voice cracking a little.

His head bobbed in a nod. "I did kill him." He straightened and took a couple of steps toward her and offered her his hand.

She didn't want the help up, but she accepted it anyway. He lifted her effortlessly to her feet, the strength in his large arms apparent.

Hesitation held her in place. She wasn't sure what he had planned now. Since he knew about her village, all she had to do was get there before he did. Maybe, hopefully, the guards would be able to defend the villagers. Brushing the leaves and dirt off her clothes, she walked with him at her heels, ready to be back with her kinsfolk.

If her mother knew she was with him, and that he possessed knowledge of their race, she'd skin Adara's hide. *Men are not to be trusted.* That was what she'd always been taught.

His furry hand closed around her elbow, and he spun her toward him. "I want you to be my mate, Adara."

Her mouth fell open, then closed. How could he just grab her without fear of death? Didn't he know Amazons were not to be treated in such a manner? Reflexively, she punched him in the jaw. Men were never allowed to touch her, but the feel of his rough palm against her flesh made tingling sensations race down her spine anew.

Yet her mind struggled to take in what he'd said. It didn't make sense. What was this about? She was taught about how some animals mated, but she had never heard of humans being mated. Then again, he wasn't human, not entirely.

"I am to be queen of the Amazons. As such, you will treat me with respect." She brushed his hand off her elbow and turned away.

2

Rei sighed and averted his gaze skyward, through the small spaces between the canopy's thick, lush foliage. Pain struck him hard, and he dropped to his knees. Bones snapped, flesh ripped and reformed, muscles realigned, and claws retracted as he willed his body to become human again. A grunt of agony slipped from his lips.

Maybe I'll be able to connect to her better this way. Sweat clung to his naked form. He climbed to his feet, watching as she walked away. Apparently, she was uninterested in the sounds of his sudden transformation… or, more likely, unwilling to betray her curiosity. Her hips swayed beneath the somewhat tattered gray material she wore in thin strips across her breasts and waist.

"Where are you going?" He had a feeling he knew. His voice was once again human and retained traces of a Siberian accent.

"Back to where I belong. My village, soon to be under my protection!" Tension tightened her already rigid posture. Her muscular, sun-bronzed back and thighs radiated with anger as she stomped ahead of him. Their motion clouded his mind and sent waves of heat through his skin. He wasn't sure why she was so upset. Maybe mentioning his desire to mate with her had set her off. He sighed. Life tended to be much simpler for his animal side. One of the things he'd enjoyed so much about being in the Amazon.

"Perhaps you should consider granting me your trust, Your Highness." He stared hard, trying to act respectful, but unsure how. "I mean, if I had wanted to kill you, I would have by now."

She twisted around and put her hands on her hips, nostrils flared. "You wouldn't have killed the person you want as your 'mate'."

* * *

Her words and anger stuck in her throat as Adara realized a tiger no longer stood before her. The beast had been replaced by a man. A man with dark brown eyes and a sensual mouth. His large build shocked her. Her kind was tall, yet he towered over her. The sight of him stole her breath. As a weretiger he was towering and intimidating, but as a man…

Even naked, he had a sophisticated, intelligent aura about him. He was much more handsome than the local Indians. They didn't have the air of confidence and grace he possessed. They bore a more savage image of life, like her people.

She shook her head, ridding herself of those thoughts. For if they were right, she had no business associating with him. All she'd known of the world had flipped upside down since meeting him.

Rei cocked an eyebrow, watching her. His gaze brushed over her, stoking the strange warmth in her belly.

Adara couldn't stop the unfamiliar heat rushing up her neck, reaching her cheeks. Her eyes lingered on his naked human form. His tan skin captured the moonlight that filtered through the very old trees.

She fought the temptation to look below his waist. Focusing on his face, she asked, "How did you do that? Change, I mean."

"How can I change? I've never truly been human. Unlike most of my kind, who were scratched or bitten, I was born this way. I can simply concentrate on the image of my body shifting, limb by limb. My body then reacts in kind, doing as I imagine. It's easy, once you get the hang of it."

Adara stood a little straighter, feeling a rebuff in his arrogant declaration of ease about something she'd thought impossible. "I see. And your family is this way too?"

"Most are. Some can't shift, but have other abilities." He glanced down at his nakedness, as if noticing it for the first time. "Hmm… I guess you're not used to seeing naked men running around here, are you? Forgive me. Shifting ruins my clothes, and they aren't very useful torn." He laughed, a smile spreading across his attractive face. "I've spent my whole life alone. I'm used to it."

"I've never seen a man like that. Naked, I mean," she sputtered, trying to fight off the blush. "My village has no men. We continue our existence by… using… male Indians from a nearby village." She shrugged, forcing her face to remain neutral as she struggled not to lower her curious gaze to his protruding shaft.

Rei raised both eyebrows this time. Another smirk started curling his lips.

"My people don't openly disclose that kind of information to just anyone. They say it's for those who are ready," Adara said. Soon, she'd experience what happens with the Indians.

Dread had filled her being when the Wise Woman had declared her and Rubia ready for the next visit. She knew she needed to perform her duty to her kind, but something about the ritual stirred up hesitation within her.

"Well, I could show you. A personalized lesson." Rei's husky voice shook her from her thoughts. Not good. She needed to focus on him or else he could jump on her again.

"What do you mean?"

"I could show you what has to happen to start new life. But you'd have to experience something else first... something pleasurable."

His words ramped up her heartbeat, causing curiosity and uncertainty to course through her veins. He reached his hand toward her.

Her eyes widened. "Leave me alone." She dodged his outstretched hand. Turning on her heel, she ran, from the words he spoke, and her own confusion. Maybe even from her desire for him.

But he was there. In front of her faster than she could comprehend. His brows were drawn together, and he held his hands up. "I'm sorry if I startled you. I didn't mean to."

"Get away from me!" She stepped back, her foot catching on an exposed root. Not again! She fell to the forest floor and hit her head on the solid ground. The last thing she saw before the world went dark was Rei reaching his hands out toward her.

3

*A*dara sat on the throne of her kingdom. Her tribeswomen stood before her, cheering their new Queen. They shouted their allegiance to her, and she raised her sword high in the air. This moment truly made her feel worthy of her title.

A blur of movement caught her attention near the gates. Dozens of tigers rushed into her village, bursting out of the jungle in ferocious explosions of black, white, and orange, almost too quick for the eye to see.

She leapt to her feet. Her warriors drew their weapons and stood together to fight against the feline attack, but the tigers were too fast, too strong, and too many.

Only moments ago, she had sworn to protect her people, to guard them with her life, and now those lives were being clawed, bitten, and shredded away while she watched in horror.

Turning her face from the massacre, she noticed Rei next to her. He wielded an Amazonian sword in his hands. What was he doing with that? Was he there to help her people?

A wide, toothy grin stretched across his face as he came toward her. He pressed the blade to her throat, fisted his hand in her hair, and forced her to watch as every one of her people was murdered.

Helplessness surged through her. If only she hadn't trusted him. Why had she thought he'd be different? History had forewarned her of the cruelness men possessed.

Rei had shown his true intentions.

When her tribeswomen lay dead, and the horrific foreign beasts started gnawing on the bones of her kin, the sword slid across her throat. Pain burned her neck. Blood gushed from the cut. She clenched her hands to the wound.

A solid kick pummeled her lower back, sending her flying off the platform. Air rushed past her as she fell.

His laughter followed her, hurting worse than any blade. The ground hurled forward.

* * *

Adara awoke screaming, her lungs burning from the effort, her throat raw. She bolted upright in a soft, cozy bed, sweaty and breathless. The moist sheets clung to her skin in the Amazon heat.

She scanned her surroundings. The place had solid wooden walls like a hut within her village, but everything looked too polished and different to be her home. A sturdy table with two chairs sat in a small area near a cooking area. A shelf lined with books stood near the sleeping area. The one-room cabin exuded warmth and coziness, unlike the tension she tended to feel at home.

Her chest heaved as her breath continued to come out in pants. In a moment of remembrance, she touched her hand to her throat, tracing the spot where the kris had slid.

It was only a dream.

She snapped her head to the side as Rei's presence made the hair on the back of her neck raise up. He reclined in a plush, red chair next to the bed. He stared at her, concern etched into the lines carved into his forehead. A frown curled his lips.

"What's wrong? Don't be afraid. You fell, so I brought you to rest at my home."

She closed her eyes and shivered. How long had she been here? "What time of day is it?"

"Just after nightfall."

"What?" She leapt out of the bed and almost stumbled to the floor. Her long legs caught in the twisted blankets. She clutched the headboard to regain her balance, its solid, dark wood reassuring under her quivering fingers.

"I need to get back to my village. They are probably worried about me." As the words scratched out of her raw throat, their full weight hit her. She was going to be in so much trouble when she reached home. "I shouldn't worry them any more than I already have."

"In that case, I will accompany you. You never know what could happen in the forest."

And she knew too. Meeting him was a perfect example. Never mind the fact he'd chased her!

"No need to come along. I'll be fine." She headed for the door.

"You still don't trust me, even after I helped you?"

She shook her head and stepped outside, hopping off the porch. Her bare feet touched the cool ground. The feel of moist, uneven earth against her callused soles provided much comfort. It chased away the terrifying phantoms of her dreams. But this was real, something she could affect and even change.

Rei followed her, stopping on the porch. "I understand. After all, I'm *just* a beast." His words were harsh. A twinge of sorrow filled his eyes, but he shrugged. His spine straightened, composure regained. "Well, if you need help, don't hesitate to ask."

"How can one trust your kind? How many are there of you?" The words escaped her mouth before she could hold them in. She grimaced.

He laughed, his voice filled with bitterness. "So you mistrust me because of what I am? Fine. You think humans are the perfect race. My family died because of your kind. All we did was live peacefully. Humans came along and killed us simply because we existed, because of who we are. They killed them out of fear and rumors. I am one of only a few weretigers left."

She stared down at the ground. His words, and the pain behind them, sank into her heart. "I didn't know." How could she have?

Without warning, a hand landed on her shoulder. No warmth remained in the touch. Only a firm, solid grasp. His seething gaze pierced her. He growled, "I am not like other weretigers. I am the ultimate form of my race: the strongest, the purest of bloods. Humans destroyed us. If pure bloods die out, all the weretigers will eventually die, exterminating my race. Mine is a rare breed.

"Pure bloods were not changed into a beast with a scratch or a bite; we were *born*. We have special abilities. We are stronger, faster and more powerful than an average weretiger."

His strong hand tightened on her shoulder, causing a dull ache to form where his hand gripped. Uneasily, she realized Rei could snap her collarbone without any effort if he wanted.

She pulled her kris from its sheath and brought its point to his chest in a blur. She wanted to finally be free of him and the torrent of emotions his existence caused.

Rei gave a bitter smile, his lips curling slightly. Angst dripped from his voice. "Go ahead, do it. Humans have wiped out all I have known. Maybe you can end my suffering. Do it. Or do you lack the courage?"

Intense pain drenched his words. His kind had been wronged, but her race was not responsible. She had nothing to do with what happened to his species. How could she have? She didn't even know where Siberia was. After all, she had just met him. What could she possibly have done without having known him?

"My people have been wronged too. My ancestors were enslaved by men and killed by their diseases and swords. We have learned to survive." She trailed the kris down, so that its tip pressed against his stomach, but didn't stab him.

He grabbed the blade with his bare hands, deftly twisting it out of her grip. With the same speed that had amazed her before, he moved behind her, holding the kris against her throat. "I won't hurt you," he said softly.

11

His breath brushed her ear, sending chills down her spine, putting her body in direct conflict with her mind. "Just don't pull stunts like that."

Flashbacks of the nightmare plagued her thoughts, chasing away logic and reason. She grabbed the kris's blade, trying to get it away from her throat. The sharp edge sliced through her hands. Blood trickled along her fingers, sliding past her wrists and down her arms.

Rei pulled away in surprise and yanked the kris away, flinging it into the trunk of a nearby tree. "Why did you do that? Do you hate me so much? Do you think I'm going to hurt you?" He spun her to face him and took her right hand in his, examining the wounds, then licked them. She tried to pull her hand away, but his grip, while tender, was too strong.

Adara grimaced as his rough tongue cleaned her wounds. The sensations of his tongue exploring her fingers and palm actually felt... good. Embarrassed at her reaction, she turned her head, trying to distract herself by looking over his small cabin. "I thought you wanted to slit my throat. You did, in my nightmare. I dreamed your people killed my villagers and warriors while you forced me to stand there and watch."

He looked at her as if she'd grown two extra heads. "You think I would want you to die? Don't you listen? I have no ill will toward your people. You fascinate me. I did not harm you earlier, and I have no intention of doing so now." He gripped her chin and forced her to look at him. "Or even in the future. Besides, I have no one to call on. I am the last pure blood, and there are only ten, at most, half-breeds left." Releasing her from his hold, he sighed and wiped a hand over his face.

Averting her gaze from the confusion in his, she looked down at her palm. Only moments ago, it had been seeping blood, but now she saw healed flesh, as if nothing had happened. She gasped. "What did you do?"

"My saliva heals wounds. I was not trying to eat you," he said with a warm grin.

"All right." Her forehead wrinkled in confusion as she searched the lines in her hand for scars. Nothing, not a single mark. She shook her head, making her hair sway in long tendrils against her face. *This can't be possible. Not even the Wise Woman could heal this quick.*

"You're confused. Why? Am I not the monster you took me for?"

"I..." Adara swallowed hard. "I don't know. This is all too new, frightening." She hugged her arms to her chest and walked toward the tree line. For the first time, she took notice of her surroundings; she'd never been to this part of the forest. It was too close to town. Had to be. Her people were not allowed to go where the risk of contact with humans was too great. Her body numbed as realization dawned that she was lost. "Where are we?"

"My home," Rei answered, as though it should have been obvious.

She glared, then tilted her head to the sky and looked through the trees' magnificent canopy. "My village is that way," she said, pointing northeast. "I can find my own way home."

"I see. May I accompany you, at least part of the way?"

She ran her gaze over his body. "You need clothes."

He laughed. "Okay, wait here." It didn't take him long to get dressed. He soon reappeared in a pair of faded blue jeans and a sleeveless shirt. He held out his arms and turned so she could see the whole ensemble. "This better?"

The outfit interested her. His shirt was such a rich color of blue. Never before had she seen such perfection of shade and texture. She wanted to reach out and touch the shirt but held back, crossing her arms instead. "Yes, it is."

Rei smirked and walked over to her. "Shall we be off, Your Highness?"

"Yes, we shall. We need to travel fast." Her words came out stilted, a somber tone underlying them.

"Then lead the way, and I will follow."

Turning away from him, Adara ran in the direction she'd pointed, feeling the humid night air cling to her skin as she sprinted over the forest floor.

4

They slowed their pace upon reaching thicker foliage.

Rei's gaze lingered on the bronze expanse of her back, then trailed it lower to watch her hips sway. He wanted to run his hands over her curves and bathe them with his tongue.

Uneasiness passed through him as they headed deeper into the forest. He tried to shake it but couldn't. "Something doesn't feel right."

With a glance over her shoulder, Adara paused. "What is it?"

"I don't know. Something seems off. I can't put my finger on it." He inhaled a deep breath, then let it slide out slowly. It escaped his lips with a soft hiss. "But it smells familiar."

"Okay." She wrinkled her forehead as she looked around but continued walking.

He stopped and pulled out his serrated knife.

"What's going on?" She stepped back as her gaze met his. She unsheathed her weapon and stopped cold in her tracks.

"It's probably nothing."

He could no longer sense the telltale sounds of someone approaching with his supernatural hearing. Only the squawking of birds and screeches of monkeys. He padded a few steps ahead of her, then froze as he heard rustling.

Adara screamed.

Whirling around with knife in hand, he saw a huge puma pinning her down, its teeth bared and angled toward her throat.

"This human must be special to you, if you want her as a mate." The puma slurred and hissed as it talked, forming human words out of its beastly mouth. Tightly coiled muscles rippled beneath its dark fur, belying the effort of keeping Adara pinned and driving fear through Rei. The puma was ready to strike, and pumas were as wild and unpredictable as the forest itself.

"Kyle, what are you doing here?"

"I'm here for you. Now, put the knife away, Rei."

He lowered his knife to the ground. "Release her."

Kyle shook his head. "Not so fast. I need your attention."

Rei glanced at Adara and pride rose in his chest. She had stopped struggling, realizing her strength was no match for the puma's, but her eyes still blazed with anger and defiance. No fear showed in her features.

"What do you want?" Adara growled, her breath coming out in short pants.

Kyle stared down at her and gave a sharp, toothy grin. "Straight to the point. I like that." She glared at him, her eyes aflame with fierce contempt. "Oh, and attitude. You certainly know how to pick them, Rei."

She distracted Kyle just long enough for Rei to act. He charged the puma, diving through the air as he shifted into tiger form. His paws connected with a solid *thud*, sending Kyle flying into a tree trunk. Pausing in his assault, Rei leaned down and jerked his head toward his cabin. It was closer than her village. "Run."

She nodded in acknowledgment. Clambering to her feet, she stared at them for a moment before running away. Her legs flew in a flurry of motion, graceful as a cheetah. He watched her go, his stomach clenching. Kyle wasn't above working in groups.

Realizing what the dark forest around them could be hiding, he shifted into his tiger-man form, the same form he had been in when he introduced himself to Adara.

In a matter of moments, he had caught up with her. She wouldn't be able to outrun a werepuma. Their speed was legendary.

"I'll catch you later," Kyle shouted.

He looked back to see Kyle, leaning against a tree and holding his side, amusement filling his emerald eyes. Sweeping Adara into his arms, Rei ran toward his cabin. It would be too close for Kyle to recover before he could catch up with them. The cabin would provide some protection from Kyle, at least. Being in the open was out of the question. But Rei knew any hope that it would fully protect them was like hoping a match would keep one warm in Siberia.

Reaching his home, he pulled the door open, then kicked it closed behind him as he set Adara down. Tossing his head back, he roared, forcing his body to shift back into human form even though it had been so soon from the last two shifts. He stood by a window, sagging with the onset of fatigue and waiting for Kyle to show himself again, hoping the puma wouldn't, but knowing he would. "I won't let him hurt you."

* * *

15

"Why does he want to hurt me?" Adara's voice shook with adrenaline. Her thudding heart made her body tremble with each pounding beat. "I don't understand... I mean, what did you do to him?" she asked, settling on the bed, her legs dangling toward the floor. She watched his face closely for any sign of an answer.

"Kyle and I used to be friends. We went to university together. We came down here on assignment as biologists, but ever since he was attacked and turned into a werepuma, his behavior has been rather unpredictable." Regret passed over Rei's face. "I don't know..." He paused, as though the memories tore through him deep inside. "I wish I had been able to protect him," he said, resting his head against the wall. His eyes focused as he opened them to meet her gaze.

"So he sees this as an opportunity for revenge?" She wrinkled her forehead.

"Well, he won't hurt you. I won't let him."

"I can defend myself."

"Yes, but not against what he is. I know you're strong, but he could get the upper hand and kill you. That's how he is. He wants me to suffer."

Adara wrapped the velvety blanket from the bed around her; its warmth made her feel safer, more peaceful. Holding it close, she said, "I can't see why he'd want to hurt you."

He sat down beside her. "As long as I draw breath, he will not harm you."

"But if you die..."

He spoke with forceful conviction, his words more a declaration of will than a statement. "Then I won't die."

"Okay." Pausing, she looked at him. "What about my people, then? He could try to kill them. We need to get to them." Jabbing her thumb into her chest, she said, "I need to get to them."

His jaw clenched. "I know we have to protect them, but until he backs off, we can't get there. He might have more of his kind with him. His kind can wait on tree branches for days until they find an opportunity to strike. His kind has survived whereas mine is nearly extinct. Tigers always have been stronger, but pumas are quicker."

"My Amazons are not weak. We can defend ourselves. We have been doing so for many years before you came along. When the men traveled down our river, they killed many of my people. The ones they didn't kill, they enslaved. Some of my people were able to stay out of sight, so we were considered a dead race, yet we have lived on and fought for survival." Adara stared down at her hands and added, "Maybe our peoples are more similar than we think."

"Maybe." He nodded in acknowledgment.

"Good, as long as we understand each other." Adara watched Rei lie back on the bed. She stood and walked to the window where he had been.

He was there in an instant, his movements so swift, she didn't even see him approach. "Don't go near the windows until we know it is safe." Drawing the drapes closed, he turned to look at her.

She stood there wrapped in the blood-red blanket, her eyes wide. "Why?"

"Because, Adara, they will be watching and waiting for a moment to attack, studying our vulnerabilities." He put his hands on her shoulders and gingerly shook her, an intense look in his eyes.

She tried to break free, but he was too strong. "Let me go, Rei."

He bent his mouth to her neck and placed a kiss over her frantic pulse, then wrapped his left arm around her waist, massaging her muscled back through the blanket. "I won't hurt you." He pulled back enough to look her in the eyes.

His rich amber eyes caught the light from the lamp, drawing her deeper into his gaze. She searched them for hidden answers, and when she found none, a soft sigh escaped her lips. "What do you have to do for me to be your mate?" she asked, the muscles in her shoulders tense.

Rei placed a finger over her lips and stroked her cheek with the back of his hand, his knuckles trailing along her jaw. "I'll show you."

She closed her eyes. His warm breath caressed her skin, his sweet words seducing their way into her ear, weaving their way through her brain. Relaxing a little, she let her arms drift around his neck, as if they had a mind of their own, almost... naturally.

He stood straighter and picked her up, cupping her thighs in his hands. His mouth found its way to her lips as her legs encircled his waist. She didn't fight him this time. He pulled back and said, "Open your mouth for me and relax, precious."

Adara leaned her mouth forward to press it against his, and his tongue swept across hers. Her hands tightened on his shoulders, and she let out a gasp. "Rei."

Rei strode over to the bed and laid her down. Locking his gaze to hers, he licked his lips in anticipation.

The look in his eyes almost made her fearful. It was so intense, as if he was hungry, and she was food. She crawled away until her back pressed against the headboard. Her pulse raced, and her mind swam. There was no denying she was frightened, but some small, niggling part within her cared about him and wanted more. Rei said he wouldn't hurt her, so she had to trust he was not lying.

Rei watched her with the same intensity a wild animal uses for its prey. He grabbed her ankles and pulled until she lay flat on her back. If he didn't touch her soon, she was going to go insane. He slid his hands up her legs, past her knees, and continued moving his palms up her thighs until he reached her small skirt.

He pushed the material up so it bunched around her waist, leaving nothing between his hands and the apex of her legs. Moving his hands to the material covering her breasts, he slipped it off, revealing her luscious flesh.

"Rei, what do you want me to do?"

"Sit up, sweetheart," he said, taking both of her wrists to help her into a sitting position. He stripped away her meager skirt, leaving her fully naked.

Adara played with the hem of his shirt before lifting it over his head. Her gaze dropped down to his pants, and her hands followed as her eyes drank in all that lay before her.

He held her hands and pushed her back. "No, I'll do it." He slid his hands down her torso and nudged her legs apart, then leaned in to kiss her belly button, her silken skin soft against his lips. Slipping his tongue out, he swirled it around the outside of her belly button before inching his way up to her breasts. He ran his tongue over her nipple, flicking it back and forth. It hardened under his touch as he brought it into his mouth, sucking hungrily. A contented murmur escaped his lips as he closed his eyes.

She grabbed his shoulders. "Rei!" Her nails dug in until pain teased his senses.

"Everything is going to be okay. I promise." Unzipping his pants, he tossed them aside, his shaft naked, hard and ready.

Her eyes were wide, and she reached out her hand to touch him. He rolled her onto her stomach and lifted her pelvis so her lower body was in the air and her head was on the pillow.

"Rei?" She felt odd about this, but a strange attraction for this man overwhelmed her too. Her thoughts fell away as his finger entered her. She dug her fists into the pillow and gasped as he sped up his finger's thrusting.

He inched his way from her moist, tight sheath, trailing his damp finger over her silken skin. Cupping his penis, he pressed it against her moist pussy. She tensed beneath him; feeling her tension, he massaged her lower back to soothe her. "Relax," he said, pressing himself inside her.

She gripped him snugly. Soft whimpers escaped her lips. "Adara, are you okay?"

"Yes. Rei, yes." Her words slid out between pants; her skin flushed red with heat. Her nails gripped the pillows, sheets, bed—whatever she could sink her fingers into. Adara had been unsure about this mating business, but Rei was very tender with her. His gentleness, despite the hunger she'd seen in his eyes, spoke to her.

They merged into one. Their bodies slickened with perspiration, the humidity of the dense forest and their own anticipation making them sweat. Their pulses pounded against the skin that held them captive, like great drums beating across a distance.

She screamed out incoherent words. Her eyes closed as she neared release.

He dug his fingers into her hips, pulling her onto him faster. She took all he offered her, her body pliant and willing. He grunted his pleasure. Her sheath clenched and trembled in release, driving him wild, and sending him bucking against her naked flesh. Chill bumps covered her skin, despite the heat of the oppressive, humid jungle.

No longer holding back, he released his seed, spilling deep within her. He rolled to his side and wrapped his arms around her. She lay there quietly. "Are you okay, sweetheart?"

"Yes, I…" She paused, her swollen lips parted. "It was wonderful." Adara snuggled against him, their nude bodies clinging together.

"I need you," he whispered into her silken hair.

5

Rei awoke slowly with Adara in his arms, her rich scent buried deep in his nostrils. Sensing a subtle shift in the air, he squeezed her warm body tight for a moment. He rolled out of bed, careful not to wake her, and walked to the window. Shoving aside the drapes, he saw Kyle standing at the edge of the clearing. He knew they needed to talk.

They stared at each other until Adara started fidgeting behind him. Hearing her whimper in her sleep, he turned away from the window. One of her hands stretched across the bed as if searching for his body. She'd wake up if he didn't go back to her, and she needed sleep after all she'd been through.

He glanced back out the window to find the clearing empty. Letting out a soft breath, he closed the curtains. Kyle wouldn't harm them, for tonight at least. When they had looked into each other's eyes from across the clearing, an understanding had passed between them. He had no idea how this change had happened. It startled him, but he'd get no answers to his questions any time soon.

Easing back on the bed, Rei grinned as Adara's arms found him. He enjoyed being so close to her, especially after all the days he'd spent watching her from a distance. Having her in his arms was more than worth dying for, if it came to that. Like breathing or water, she was very much a necessity. He kissed her softly on the lips.

* * *

Adara opened one eye to make sure Rei was asleep. When she was convinced, she opened the other eye and slid up his body to return the kiss without waking him. A smile spread across her lips at what they had shared last night.

She sprawled out next to him and was pulled back into dreamland.

Once again, she was on her throne before her people, but this time Rei stood next to her, and she had a rounded belly, both of them smiling. He had a glimmer of pride in his eyes.

Soon, she would bear his child. A new experience, yet one she enjoyed. Everyone in the village was happy. They hadn't been sure about Rei at first, but they had quickly warmed to the idea of having him around. It was a major change in their customs. She was queen now, so she was in charge of doing what was right for her people and the village she loved.

Everything was perfect, almost too much so. She frowned. This was all going surprisingly well. There had to be some unknown drawback or danger lurking close by. Even in her dreams, she didn't have power to fight the darkness before it was too late.

Her gaze stayed focused on Rei, and no matter how hard she tried, she couldn't look away from him to scope out their surroundings. She opened her mouth to tell someone, but no sound came out. Adara put her hands to her throat. She was helpless, and nothing she did would help.

Adara's eyes opened, and she glanced around the room. Something had awakened her. She reached across the bed to see if Rei had been roused from sleep too. Her hand brushed his chest.

She rolled over and stared at the perfection of his body. She wanted to run her tongue over him in the most intimate of ways. Her body tightened at the thought of their union, and she wanted more.

* * *

Rei sniffed the air, smelling Adara's arousal. He ran a finger up her taut body, from belly button to mouth. She was the most beautiful woman he'd ever seen, and she was all his. He wet his lips with a sweep of his tongue and stared into her eyes.

She leaned in to kiss him. As he slid his hand into her long silky hair, a sudden shift of air currents interrupted his thoughts, and that could signify only one thing. He pulled away from Adara and swung out of bed, wrapping a robe around his body. He crossed the small living area to the door in a blink of an eye, opened it, and saw Kyle standing in the entrance.

"Are you alone?" Rei asked.

"Yes, I am." Kyle folded his arms over his chest, not moving from where he stood.

"What are you doing here?"

"We need to talk."

Rei glanced over his shoulder at Adara. She sat on the bed with the covers pulled to her chin. "Wait a moment." He shut the door and walked toward her.

"Why is he here?" she asked.

"He wants to talk, sweetheart."

"Are you sure this is safe?" she whispered, pressing her cheek to his chest, exposed between the two dark folds of the robe.

"If he was going to attack, he would have already. Besides, I won't let him hurt you." Rei stroked a hand through her sultry blonde hair. He enjoyed feeling her in his arms and wished Kyle hadn't shown up. *It must be important, or else he wouldn't be here.*

"Get dressed and go in the back... please," he said, tugging on his jeans. She put on her clothes and walked into the back room, where the small bathroom was.

He opened the door again to find Kyle still standing there, one eyebrow raised.

"You sent your woman away." Kyle walked in with a smirk as Rei stepped aside.

"I'm cautious, especially after yesterday."

"That's acceptable," Kyle said. "Is she okay?"

Rei dipped his head in a nod. "What do you want to talk about?" He watched Kyle warily as he paced, looking for any sudden movement that could mean an attack. Knowing Kyle's strength and ferocity, Rei couldn't completely relax. He had to be ready for anything. A slight shift of weight might mean incoming attack.

"Your life may be in danger, and you are now... a protector and a mate." There was a solemnity to his words, which seemed almost out of place. This whole conversation seemed out of place. But then again, he wasn't sure what to think about Kyle after yesterday.

"How do you know I'm in danger?" Rei asked.

"I found out from one of my men. They are jealous of your mating with the princess. They believe, by killing you, they have a chance with her."

"But the laws—"

"They're young and don't want to follow laws. You should be careful. I'll keep an eye out."

"What about yesterday?" Rei asked.

"I wanted to get your attention. I was finally able to catch you and wanted to make things clear. But I didn't mean any harm. Now I must go, so watch your back."

Rei didn't know what to say. "You too."

6

Rei walked toward the door to the back room. It opened slowly as he approached.

"Is it safe to come out?" Adara asked.

"Yes, sweetheart, it is," he said with a faint smile playing on his lips. She was stunning. Her long, blonde hair looked soft as silk, while her body was firm, yet feminine in all the right places.

He'd never leave her. She was his everything, and he wanted to always be with her, no matter what that meant. He'd do anything to keep her happy. Anything to keep her safe.

Rei wrapped an arm around her waist and hugged her tight. Staring at her now, in such close proximity to her, he wanted to finish what they had started earlier, but it was time for her to go home. It'd be good for her, and she would be able to calm her people's fears. Something she needed to do.

How would they react to him? A few days ago, he had chased down their soon-to-be queen and now was mated with her. He didn't know what he'd do if they tried to keep her from him. Perhaps he would kidnap her in the middle of the night. Her people could not be told the truth of these last few days. He did not want to let her go. There was too great a chance of losing her.

"Adara," he said suddenly. "When we go back to your village, we won't mention anything that has occurred, right? I don't think your people would favor me."

He watched as her face grew thoughtful. She knew her people better than he did. Surely, between the two of them, they would figure something out for the best of their future together.

"I guess it wouldn't be wise since men aren't looked upon highly in my tribe. We fear men will try to overpower us again, to kill us, or enslave us. And the last few days would really make them dislike you, even more than they might normally," she said.

"Do you regret what we've done?" he asked.

"Of course not. I was suspicious of you, but then I saw a new side of you. I feel more contented now." She smiled and put her head against his chest, a blush caressing her cheeks.

"Thank you." He felt some relief from her words, but that didn't completely quell his nervousness of what her people would do when, or if, he met them. "Want to begin the journey now to your village?"

* * *

Adara nodded. She had to see to the wellbeing of her people. The time spent with Rei at his cabin was wonderful, but her people counted on her and were surely worried for her safety. It wasn't proper to be gone this long without telling someone first. That was how some of the women had died. She wrapped her arms around his waist and kissed his chest.

She glanced at him as he slid his arms around her shoulders.

"I don't know if we should do this," Rei said. "We may never make it to your village."

She pulled away from him and strode to the table, retrieving her kris and sheath. She secured it in place and turned to see Rei tugging on a burgundy shirt to go with his jeans. She smiled and walked over to the door. "Shall we go?"

"Yes." He opened the door for her, and they walked outside into the bright, humid day side-by-side.

Adara tossed a sidelong glance in Rei's direction. He looked as though he was gathering his confidence. Her gaze turned to watch the rain of leaves that never ceased in this forest. She listened to the normal quiet silence of the Amazon rainforest and felt at home. It was the only time when silence was not a sign of fear.

In all of the times she'd wandered off to walk the forest, she always appreciated being an Amazon, not that she'd really thought of life outside the jungle. It was so beautiful here.

His hand found hers, and they walked through the forest to her village. Everything was peaceful and serene. No danger was in the air, just comfortable companionship with Rei.

Gradually, her surroundings became more recognizable. They closed in on her village. The walk was soon going to end. She slowed, knowing she needed to think of what she was going to tell her people, and he matched her pace.

The village, with its wooden barriers and walkways that hung from the trees and gave the Amazons a better chance to defend against enemies, soon came into view. "We are very near, Rei," Adara murmured as they stepped into the covering of a large tree to hide, not ready to face her people. They needed to keep their distance between the sentries posted here and there along the wall until then.

"I'm aware of that. No matter what happens now, please know I care for you. Nothing will change that."

"I care about you too." She wrapped her arms around his neck and they kissed. It was fiery, as if this would be the last time they would be able to, and maybe it was. She wanted this to be memorable.

Rei wrapped his fingers into her hair and drew her head away from his. "It's time. I can't wonder about our fate any longer. The burden weighs heavy on my heart."

Adara nodded and tilted her chin in the air. She would not cry. Not yet. Going back around the large tree, she walked toward the village gate. Two Amazon lookouts stood on the walkway above the gate to the village. They must have noticed her too. They pointed and signaled to others on the ground. They yelled and called others to the gate.

She raised her kris in the air, and they immediately raised their swords, acknowledging her as one of them. Glancing over her shoulder, she saw that Rei was still behind her. She continued her walk to the village. She wanted to get there before he did, so not all of the initial attention would go toward him.

When Adara reached the gate, her mother and grandmother waited there, along with most of the villagers. They swarmed her, giving her hugs and firm words laced with concern and loyalty.

When everyone calmed down, Adara held her hand out to Rei. She heard gasps, as if no one had seen him until that moment. It was good to be back with her friends and family, but hopefully they would understand Rei was part of her life now too.

"Mother," Adara began, "I have something to tell you. Something important to me and the cause of my absence. This is Rei. I don't think I could live without him." He stiffened beside her, obviously as uncomfortable with the situation as she was.

Adara couldn't help but squirm, waiting for her judgment under her mother's intense gaze.

"We shall discuss this further after you have rested, my child." Her mother glanced toward Rei as if measuring him up.

As they went through the gates of the village, the villagers scattered back to their work while Adara, her mother and Rei went to her mother's home to talk in private.

Tension was high, but they would get through it. There was no going back now.

7

Adara, Rei and her mother sat around her mother's short wooden table on the mats laid out on the floor. A thick wave of silence filled the air around them, carrying the tension. What would her mother say? What could she say?

Her mother waved her hand at Rei. "How did you meet this... man?"

"I was walking through the forest when we..." Adara paused and glanced at Rei, who frowned. "Bumped into each other."

Mother stared at her with an eyebrow raised. "You bumped into each other? In the middle of the forest? I see."

Adara nodded. It sounded silly now, but it was almost the truth. They had met while she was walking through the forest. "Yes, Mother."

"You do care for him, so I could not change that even if I wanted to. I must rely on your judgment to make the best choice for you and the people of this village." She stood regally, shifting her gaze between the two of them. "This is a decision for you to make, my daughter. Look inside your heart, for there lies the answer. When you have had time to think this over, then we will talk again." Her gaze shifted to Rei. "Don't harm my daughter and don't bring attention to yourself, for the people of our village know no trust when it comes to men. Depending on the answer she gives, you may or may not be welcome here. It was once against our laws to have a man in the village. If the princess declares it, so then it will be." She nodded her head to them, leaving them alone.

Adara and Rei exchanged a glance. They were silent for a few moments. "I guess that's a good sign, right?" he said.

She nodded. "I guess so. You haven't been attacked."

He grinned. "Don't jinx it."

"I think we should discuss this subject. Do you really want me as your mate?"

26

He blinked in surprise. "Being your mate is not something I can do until I don't want to anymore. It's a lifetime commitment. What don't you understand?" He ran his fingers through his rich black hair, sighing. "I care for you more than someone with such a bleak existence should be able to. You've brought a light to my life."

Adara let his words sink in and exhaled a breath she hadn't even known she'd been holding.

"I feel the same about you, Rei." She reached out her hand and stroked his cheek. He held her hand to his face and leaned in for a kiss.

He released his hold on her hand and sunk his fingers into her hair. He kissed her tenderly in a long, sensual kiss. He pulled back, and a sigh of contentment drifted from his lips. "Adara, I can't, or I might not stop."

"I don't want to stop, either." She ran her fingertips down his chin, then across his neck and shoulders until her touches were the barest of caresses, before she put her hands in her lap.

"What has been decided, my dear?" Her mother's voice drifted through the silence, causing them to look up in surprise. She stepped into the house and shut the door behind her.

"I have my answer, Mother," she said. "I would like to have Rei as my mate."

A tense silence filled the room as her mother nodded slowly. "I honor your request, daughter. Be ready tonight for a feast to celebrate your return and to acknowledge your decision."

"Thank you." Adara hugged her.

"There is no need to thank me. The decision came from you. I cannot deny a decision from a princess's heart." Her gaze shifted from Adara to Rei. "You are welcome here since she has decreed her feelings for you. Just be cautious."

8

Adara dressed in a short, traditional dress in a nice shade of dark purple. Her grandmother had made it for her a few years ago, but she'd never had the perfect occasion to wear it.

Now was a fine time, as the village feasted in celebration of her safe return to them. Her grandmother would be happy.

She felt beautiful and gave a small spin, smiling. Everyone would love it. Her gaze slid to the doorway of her home to find Rei standing there. She wondered how long he'd been waiting.

"You look beautiful, sweetheart," he said. He wore a pair of jeans and a form-fitting black shirt. The two of them looked as opposite as night and day, but it didn't matter, did it? His hair was down and reached his shoulders. He looked sizzling.

"And you are handsome," she replied. They walked to the center of the village where a large bonfire shot sparks into the air. People were already crowding around in anticipation of the feast. It wasn't often they feasted. They didn't have many occasions to celebrate, so whenever something great happened, they did.

Rubia ran over to them. "I've missed you, Adara! Everyone was so worried. We thought you were dead. There are many dangers for one to face in the Amazon alone." Rubia was two summers younger than her and always worried, since Adara tended to get into mischief.

"Oh, Rubia! I've never gotten hurt when I went off before." Adara smiled.

She'd known her people would be worried, but everything had worked out so far. She was glad to be back, but things were different, as if her people silently fumed over her decision to remain with Rei. There was no clear evidence, but in her own way, she knew. Trouble was nearby and, added to her recent dreams, it didn't help her psyche at all.

Her thoughts focused on the dreams she'd been having. The themes of betrayal, the death of her people, and her inability to make a difference haunted her. If only she knew if and when something was going to happen, then she wouldn't feel so powerless.

Adara blinked as she heard her name. Rei and Rubia stared at her.

"Are you okay?" Rei asked.

She nodded.

Rubia stared nervously.

She frowned. "Yes, I'm fine. Why do you ask?" She looked between Rei and Rubia, running her fingers through her hair.

"We called your name, but you just stood there staring off into the distance. It was scary, Adara," Rubia said.

"I'm sorry. I have a lot on my mind." Adara looked into the trees around them and inhaled a deep breath. Movement in the trees caught her attention, but faded just as quickly. Was she going crazy? The thing she was experiencing wasn't natural.

"Well," she said, "we should find a seat by the fire before it's too late." The words sounded strange on her tongue, and she shook her head.

* * *

Rei and Rubia glanced at each other in confusion as she walked past.

"What's gotten into her?" Rubia asked from behind her.

"I have no clue. She wasn't like this before," Rei said. They followed her to the fire in silence.

Rei seated himself to her right, and Rubia to her left. They needed to pay extra close attention to their surroundings and especially to Adara. She wasn't acting right. Something had to be wrong.

Rei looked around, wondering what a feast consisted of to these Amazons. He caught glances from a few people. Murder was in their faces. The intensity of it made him want to shiver, but he would not allow them to think he was scared. He was not. He could run faster than these women, and he was stronger.

His gaze rested on Adara's mother as she walked toward them and the fire. She looked calm as always, though he felt other emotions radiate from her. Distrust. Uncertainty. Confusion. Above all that, she wore regality like a cloak. Just like Adara.

She made an announcement he didn't quite catch, but from the way the crowd responded, he could tell the feast for Adara was beginning. He kept his eyes open to his surroundings and wished they were still at his cabin. But it wouldn't be right to keep Adara holed up there for his own pleasure. Her people would miss her.

* * *

The sun began to fall as feasting continued, but Adara couldn't shake the odd feeling that something was going to happen soon. And it wasn't going to be pretty. She closed her eyes, and a sharp image of a bloody sword appeared in her mind. She opened her eyes, and her hand hovered near her kris.

Rei's knee bumped hers. She glanced over at him, and there was a question on his face. His gaze drifted down to her hand. She knew he'd gotten the message. He looked around at their surroundings.

Tension was thick in the air. Loud, feline growls reverberated in the air. And they sounded close by. Weapons appeared in several warriors' hands.

Adara leapt to her feet, staring around at the village and wondering where the attackers would come from. She couldn't shove down the fear ripping through her chest at the outcome of this battle. If it was anything like her nightmares—well, she didn't want that to be the case.

Her kris was in her hand as she scoured the area for any sign of the big cats. Out of the corner of her eye, she saw movement, then went flying through the air to land hard on her back. The tip of her kris was up, piercing the heart of the werepuma who had struck her and pinned her to the ground. Sandi, her mother's second-in-command, pushed the dead werepuma off her and reached down her hand.

Adara stared at her for a moment, blinking away the shock of the blow before accepting the help and being pulled to her feet.

"Defend the princess," Sandi called out to the other warriors, shoving her sword in the air.

Adara almost smiled, but it was too soon. More werepumas bounded through the gate toward them, Kyle leading the charge. Yells from the tower guards sent fear pulsing through her veins. Her breath came out in shallow gasps. Her nightmares were coming true.

* * *

Rei walked toward Kyle and his werepumas outside of the Amazons' hearing. "What's going on?" he asked.

"It's as I feared. They'll be here soon," Kyle said.

"What about that guy?" Rei asked and nodded to the dead werepuma.

"I thought he was reliable, but I was wrong. I'm here to help you and these women fight. It's my fault the rogue pumas know where you and your mate reside."

Rei put a hand on his shoulder. "You did what you thought was best." He glanced up to see Adara jogging toward them.

"What's going on?" she asked. Her gaze slid between them and finally landed on Rei.

"More of those rogue pumas will be along soon. Have your people ready for a fierce fight. The pumas are strong; you and your people need to be prepared," Rei said.

Her eyes widened. She looked back at her people and ran to them.

Rei watched her work as he stood with Kyle, listening to the strategies he suggested.

After a few moments, the villagers all stared at Rei and Kyle. Kyle's werepumas knelt on the ground near him, a question of "what's next" was plain in their eyes. They were ready. Why would the pumas want to harm the folks of this tribe? It didn't make sense. They were a secluded tribe and not overtly hostile. They wanted to be left alone.

He walked toward Adara with Kyle and his group following close behind.

But Kyle stopped in his tracks. He let out a low growl. "They're here," he said in a whispered tone.

Rei nodded. He'd known Kyle a long time, as both friend and enemy, but he was glad they were no longer enemies since Kyle had been quite a formidable one. He turned to Adara and kissed her on the lips, then leaned back until his lips hovered just above hers. "They are here." He locked his gaze with hers, examining her features and finding no fear.

His heart turned over with pride. They were about to go up against powerful creatures, which were stronger and faster than her, but if she was afraid, she hid it well. His gaze drifted over to Rubia and saw a similar look. These Amazon women were truly extraordinary.

He turned back to face Kyle. It was time. Adara signaled her people with a loud whistle behind him as the rogue pumas started swarming through the gates toward them. He shifted his hands from fingers to claws, making sure his body was firmly in front of Adara's so she would come to no harm.

Apparently, Adara had a different plan. She stepped beside him and lashed out with her kris at the nearest werepuma. He didn't feel comfortable with her fighting them.

"Adara!" he shouted as a werepuma tackled her from the side. The one who fought him moved in a fury of claws and fangs, almost too quick for him to keep up with. He transformed into his half-man, half-tiger form. His heart raced, and he tossed the werepuma into the large bonfire. It shrieked and hissed in pain and agony. He had to get to Adara. The werepuma that had tackled her had his teeth slowly closing in on her neck as she shoved against his beastly chest.

Was she going to be able to defend herself? Would the beast kill her? Could he even get to her in time to protect her? He cast a glance over at her again. She still fought with the werepuma. Rei ripped his claws through his other opponent's throat, severing muscles and arteries. The puma gurgled

31

and squealed in anguish until his cries were only soft whimpers.

Rei ran to Adara's side. He grabbed her adversary by the throat and squeezed, crushing its windpipe and suffocating the werepuma to death. He let its body fall from his strong grip. It plopped to the ground like a rejected doll. Closing his eyes, he forced his body back into his human form, gritting his teeth against the intense pain that shook him as his bones and joints broke and realigned. He was panting when a hand touched his shoulder. Swirling around, he gripped the owner's throat, but it was Kyle.

Rei's hand fell away from his throat. "I'm sorry," he said, sucking in a breath.

"It's okay, my friend," Kyle said, clearing his throat and rubbing his neck. He played it down. A few rogue werepumas still fought, but they were being easily subdued by the combined strength of the Amazons and Kyle's pumas. The villagers nearby were staring at Rei. A quiet hush spread through the air.

He took in another deep breath, then his gaze sought Adara. She was staring at him with her chest rising and falling at a rapid pace. He had no clue what she was thinking. He could hardly take his gaze from her tempting breasts. They taunted him, seduced him. Carnal hunger surged through his body, and he needed to take her somewhere private.

From the corner of his eyes, he saw Kyle and Rubia talking. They both smiled, and a spark ignited between them. Maybe Kyle would finally find peace and happiness with Rubia. Rei certainly hoped so. Kyle had risked his life by saving theirs.

He turned his gaze back to see Adara standing before him. "I was afraid for you," he said.

Adara smiled, and it lit up her face. He loved her.

"I can tell. From the speed and strength you fought with, I'm grateful you were with us Amazonians. I love you, Rei," she said, wrapping her arms around his waist and resting her head against his chest.

He held her close. "Adara," he began breathlessly, "we need to go somewhere private." He pulled her back from his body, looking into her eyes.

Her eyes widened, and she nodded. "Yes, but I need to make sure all is well with my village first." They walked over to Adara's mother, where Kyle and Rubia already stood.

"Mother, how are things with the village? Is there a need of my presence? I would like to retire to my home." She kept her gaze straight on her mother.

"You fought bravely, my child. Sandi is handling clean-up of the village, if you'd like to assist, but no, I don't see a need for you to stay." Her gaze swept to Rei and then back to Adara. "After talking with Kyle, we will set forth a treaty between the village and the werepumas for the protection of all, but we'll handle that tomorrow. Go rest, dear one. You will be alerted when it's time."

"Thank you," Adara said. She bowed her head, then walked toward her home with Rei at her heels. "Won't this look obvious?"

"I'm not worried about being obvious, sweetheart," he said huskily. He opened the door to her home, then barricaded it after they had entered.

* * *

She watched him, and her breath caught in her throat as he turned toward her. She wrapped her arms around his neck, then was lifted into his arms.

He stared at her as if she were the only thing in the whole world that mattered. His lips brushed against hers, causing goose bumps to careen down her arms. She opened her mouth to the sweeping invasion of his kiss.

Rei set her onto the firmness of her bed and leaned over her. His breath was hot on her skin where his lips hovered above. He sat her up and pulled her dress over her head.

Adara's fingertips fluttered down his chest until they approached the hem of his shirt. She yanked it over his head, baring his perfect chest. Her hands went to the button of his jeans, and she unbuttoned it. He grabbed her wrists, causing a gasp to escape her mouth. He leaned her back and placed her hands beside her head with a smile.

She raised an eyebrow, turning his smile into a grin. He slid his pants down. Her breath caught in her throat. His shaft was large and firm. It made her feel beautiful that he reacted to her this way.

He blanketed her body with his and trailed kisses from the corner of her mouth down to the frantic pulse in her neck. A strong pull tugged in her lower regions, and she whispered his name.

He pulled her nipple into his mouth and cupped her breast. His teeth grazed the perky bud, causing her to arch her back.

She wrapped her arms around him and cried out, "Rei! Please!"

His breath against her skin felt achingly hot. He pushed his cock into her pussy, filling her until she thought she couldn't hold any more of him.

He moved inside her in slow, seductive motions. Their tongues sparred in the fury of their kiss. Rei picked up his pace to strong, hard strokes until she wondered if they would truly become one.

Pressure began to form in the pit of her belly until she writhed in ecstasy, sending Rei over the edge with her. Her lips brushed his as he rolled to the side. They were pressed so close together because of her small bed. It was amazing to be with him like this.

"I love you, Rei." Her voice came out breathily.

"I love you too."

9

Adara awoke with a start. She was alone on her empty, narrow bed. She reached out and touched the spot where Rei had lain next to her. Still warm.

His presence hadn't been a dream after all. Her gaze darted to her door to find it still barricaded. So he hadn't left her hut.

A small huff sounded in the room. Her attention dipped over the side of the bed to see him lying beside it on his back. His eyes were closed.

"Rei," she whispered, "are you awake?"

His eyes flashed open. He surged into a sitting position, scanning his surroundings as if confused about where he was, until his gaze connected with hers. A smile slid across his face. "Hi."

A knock pounded on the door. "Adara, it's time to get up," Rubia called. "You're needed for the ceremony."

"One moment!" Heat rushed up her neck and burned her face. Relief swept through her that Rei had blocked the door. Rubia probably would have walked right in. She wasn't one to knock first; but then again, there hadn't been a need to before. There certainly was one now.

She'd need to talk to Rubia about knocking first, or putting some kind of lock on her door like Rei had at his place.

Adara scrambled out of bed and tripped over Rei. He caught her before she could smack against the hard wooden floor of her hut. He dragged her down beside him and rolled so his body blanketed hers, leaving her breathless. Her chest heaved, trying to get in as much oxygen as she could.

His lips slid over her jaw and across her throat. His hand brushed over her breast and down her side to her hip. His attention made her heart pound that much faster.

If she gave into him, she wouldn't be able to stop. Not something they needed to be getting into right now.

Another knock interrupted the moment. She nudged Rei off her and pulled on the fancy dress she'd been wearing. Her gaze slid to Rei.

He tugged his jeans over his delicious buttocks and trim hips. He was fully aware of his body and just how good he looked. Another blush warmed her cheeks as he looked over his shoulder at her and grinned.

He had done that for her reaction. *Argh!*

Adara went to the door and slid the barricade away from it. Peeking outside into the bright day, she saw Rubia standing there with her hands on her hips, her spine stiff. She slipped out of her home, not wanting to deal with this at the moment.

"Sorry," Adara said, smiling to help calm her down.

Rubia looked at her with suspicion plain in her eyes. "Why couldn't I open the door? What was going on in there? And why did it take so long for you to come to the door when your hut is so small?"

"My! You're full of questions," Adara said, but the truth was, she didn't want to answer.

Rubia didn't look amused. "Adara—" Her words were cut off, and her gaze shot behind her, eyes widening with surprise.

Adara flinched and slowly turned to see Rei standing behind her with the look of a contented cat on his face. Frowning, she turned back to Rubia. A look of disbelief slid across Rubia's face, and her eyes were all for Adara.

Rubia's eyes widened even more, the whites of her eyes clearly visible. "What?" She'd have to learn soon enough about a man's touch. The next time the Indians came to their village, she'd be one of the chosen to lie with a man.

Adara shook her head, biting her lower lip. Not wanting to think about that. "Nothing." At least she had found someone to lie with. She wouldn't be forced to mate with anyone besides Rei. That thought eased some of the tension that built within her chest.

The three of them walked to the queen's platform, where everyone else had already gathered around. It looked like they were the last ones in the entire village to arrive.

Mother probably wasn't happy to be kept waiting.

"Amazons, today is a special day. I feel it is time that I step down for our princess, Adara, to be crowned Queen. She is better suited to handle this new era, and she shall conduct the peace agreement with the werepumas' leader, Kyle." Adara's mother spoke from her throne. Her face was strict, but when their eyes met, pride shone in her eyes—something Adara hadn't thought she'd see.

A warm breeze blew across her face. She was amazed that her mother was doing this now. She had wanted to be queen, but never imagined actually having all that responsibility. *Am I ready for this?*

Adara's mother noticed them and waved her over. "Come, my daughter. You shall now be crowned the Queen of the Amazons." A smile of pride made her face shine as Adara stepped onto the platform. Yet a cold chill ran down Adara's spine.

She took a deep breath and exhaled. She faced her mother as the customary words were spoken over her. Her mother lifted the delicate crown from her head and placed it on Adara's.

She turned to face her people and shoved her kris in the air. Cheers rang out through the village, yet she only had eyes for Rei. He was standing a little off from the crowd and smiling. She sat on her throne, and Sandi, her new second-in-command, led Kyle onto the platform.

Sandi stood next to Adara and crossed her arms over her chest. "Present your terms."

"My people can help protect your Amazons against an attack of other werekin. In return, I'd like my people to have a chance to procreate with your women." Kyle's attention drifted over to Rubia before returning to Adara and Sandi.

Murmurs rose from the crowd.

Adara opened her mouth to respond, but Sandi got there first. "That's fine about lending your strength, but we already have a source of reproduction."

"I'd like to add that if the feelings are mutual, then I see no reason for your men to not find pleasure with my people." She glanced up at her new second-in-command to see Sandi raise her eyebrow and shrug. "We will offer your werepumas the same in return."

"Are you in agreement?" Sandi said to Kyle.

He nodded. "I am."

"It is set then by your words. If this agreement is broken…" The solid muscles in Sandi's arms flexed in warning.

"It won't be." Kyle's gaze wandered back to the crowd.

When the agreement was completed, the festivities began.

Rubia blushed as Kyle walked toward her with a grin of the cat finding the cream. She had such an innocent curiosity for Kyle.

Adara walked toward Rei, smiling at the two of them. "Do you see the way they're looking at each other?"

"There's something there. Kyle doesn't show feelings easily," he said.

She hadn't known what to think about Kyle since their first meeting with him. Kyle had acted so peculiar, but he'd done something that had protected her people. She wrapped her arms around Rei and rested her head on his chest. Life before Rei had been so dull. She was so happy to have him by her side.

EPILOGUE

A dara sat on her throne with her belly swollen. Rei's child grew within her womb. She ran her hand over her stomach idly as she watched her people.

Fingertips massaged her shoulder, and she smiled. Rei brought a warmth and happiness she'd never experienced before.

Gazing out at the celebration of her pregnancy, she locked her eyes on her best friend. How would their relationship hold up now that she was queen and had a mate? Would they still venture out and have fun?

Adara sighed, knowing that her time wouldn't be as free, but she'd try her best to keep their relationship strong. Besides, who said adventure didn't bring about good things? If she hadn't ventured into the jungle alone that night, her life might not include Rei in it now.

Rei's lips brushed the top of her head as she continued to watch the crowd. To her right, one of the elders frowned and wrinkled her nose. Yet another hurdle they needed to cross. Public affection.

Kyle sidled up next to Rubia and spoke something into her ear. Her eyes widened, and a blush reddened her cheeks as she cut her gaze to him. A smirk spread across his face. Lust filled his eyes.

Adara laughed. Something bright would fill their futures.

Rei's massaging fingers slightly tightened on her shoulder. She glanced up at him. He wore a mischievous smile that caused heat to spread up her skin. Obviously, he'd caught what Kyle had done as well.

She cocked an eyebrow at him.

He chuckled and kissed her forehead. Then his gaze turned back to the crowd below, lips still quirked.

The traditions of her people were changing. Rei was one of her advisors now, but she kept close counsel with her second-in-command and the Wise Woman. That part, she would never change. Her village, though strong and isolated, needed to remember where they came from. Their people wouldn't survive further attack, not even with the help of the shapeshifters.

Her people's numbers had lowered far too much. Female children weren't born to them as often as male children. And it was against their custom to keep males in their village. Then again, she wasn't exactly sure how things would be now. Rei and the other shapeshifters didn't reside with her people in the village. Instead, they visited frequently, and when no one was looking, snuck in for midnight passion. But would that change in the near future?

Not everything could be decided at once. Thought and discussion were needed. Not only with the shapeshifters, but also with the Indian men who were beginning to be pushed aside and no longer needed for her people to become impregnated. How would they react?

She shook the thoughts from her mind and focused on the event. Celebrations occurred more often. The werepumas were invited to join their feasts too. They even offered prey to be cooked—something her people weren't used to. No one provided for them. They had to provide for themselves.

Couplings slowly began to form between Amazon women and the werepumas, making the mingling of the sexes a little more tolerable in Amazonian standards. Although not everyone was quick to join the cause.

The elders refused to acknowledge this change, yet they displayed enough compassion to let their younger tribeswomen decide the path they wished to travel. After all, her generation would be the protectors of their race, so they would still have a future.

War between the sexes didn't trouble her mind anymore. Danger didn't come from gender, but from those with the desire to do harm. She had found that there wasn't only violence in a man's touch. A pleasurable passion existed there as well, one able to catapult a woman into another world altogether.

JUNGLE FIRE

1

Rubia Costa tied down her hammock in a peaceful spot where she went to get away. She'd told no one of this spot, and yet she was within yelling distance of her people. Help would come if the need arose.

She didn't dare venture far from her village. But these days, her village wasn't as calm and mundane as it once had been. So far, she wasn't sure whether that was good or bad. Life and traditions were changing, and she couldn't hold back her confusion as pieces of what she'd been taught now unraveled around her.

She climbed onto the hammock and gazed at the trees above her. The hammock swung gently, lulling her into the relaxed state she so desired. She closed her eyes and sighed softly.

The dream world rose up to greet her. The sound of dry leaves crunching underfoot forced her back to alertness. Her eyes shot open to see a tall, dark-haired man staring at her.

She lunged for her spear, stuck in the ground nearby. Gradually, the realization dawned on her who this man was, and she settled back, her nerves still tense and ready to fight.

"Some reflexes you have there," Kyle Reynolds said. A grin stretched across his lips, brightening his face. At ease, he leaned against the tree near her feet while she admired his broad, muscular shoulders that narrowed down to a slim waist.

She rolled her eyes and crossed her arms, unwilling to show the impact his presence had on her. "What are you doing here? How did you find me?"

"My sense of smell isn't as acute as other animals', but it's good enough to find where you went. I wanted to make sure you're not out getting in trouble." His grin turned into a smirk, and he pushed off from the tree.

"What? Like my friend…" She grimaced. Although they still talked,

Adara had so much going on. They didn't spend as much time together as they had before, especially now with Rei in Adara's life.

"I don't know what you're talking about." He winked and sat next to her in the hammock. It tilted enough that she slid closer to him.

Her hip bumped his, and her nerves tingled. She crawled away. Unfortunately, he must have taken that as an invitation to come closer, since he lay next to her. "What are you doing? Get out of my hammock." She scooted farther away as her body started to slip toward his once again.

Kyle grabbed her wrist and kissed her knuckles. His gaze held something she'd seen in glances between Rei and Adara. Those kinds of emotions were unfamiliar to her. Vaguely, she realized their meaning, but why would Kyle project that toward her?

He trailed his lips over her wrist and slowly moved up her arm. His warm breath tickled her flesh. She couldn't drag her gaze from his. Her voice escaped in a whisper. "What are you doing?"

"Something I've wanted to do for a while now. You don't make this easy for me, Rubia." He rolled over carefully. His body hovered over hers, and he pressed his lips against her shoulder and then her neck.

Sensations of pleasure spread between her legs, warming her body to a fever pitch. What were they doing? Panic rose up within her, and she shoved hard at Kyle's chest, throwing him off balance. The hammock tilted, and air rushed by just before her body hit the ground with a thud.

Pain throbbed throughout her back, and a groan welled from her throat. She blinked her eyes open.

Kyle knelt next to her. Concern etched soft lines at the corner of his mouth. "Are you okay?"

The ache in her back sharpened, and she fought not to wince. Instead, she pushed against Kyle's chest. "I'm fine. I can walk."

Kyle stared at her with a raised eyebrow. He shook his head. "I'll carry you. It's no trouble."

Great. She didn't want her tribeswomen to see him carting her around as if he was her protector or had… claimed her. Let alone the state she was in. They might worry she'd been injured, which wasn't far from the truth since she wasn't feeling too well at the moment.

She shoved against him, but it was like trying to move a solid tree trunk. He didn't budge an inch. Her people had studied the werecats, since they lived in such close proximity, but she had a hard time getting used to one being so close. She wasn't sure she wanted to be intimate with Kyle.

Something about him was alluring, but she couldn't dream of becoming tied to the werepumas' leader and shirking her responsibilities as an Amazon. She wanted to lead a peaceful, simple life. Those words were foreign when Kyle was involved.

He stood just out of sight from the village's catwalks, and she wriggled in his arms.

"Set me down. Right now." She lowered her voice and glared at him. If only he didn't have such a solid grip on her spear, but there was no chance she'd be able to wrestle it away from him. Not if he didn't want her to.

He watched her, and his lips twisted. Determination set in his jaw, but he gently placed her feet on the ground. "Fine. Go show everyone how strong and brave you are." He muttered under his breath, "Silly woman."

Her eyes narrowed at him, and she thrust out her hand, wanting her spear back. "Don't think you can demean me. I won't tolerate such abuse."

His soft lips tightened into a thin, pink line, and he handed over her spear. "You shouldn't be alone outside of the village."

"I'm not your concern. Shouldn't you be off leading your werepumas instead of keeping me from enjoying a moment's peace alone?" Her fist clenched around the sturdy wooden shaft, and she straightened her spine to her full height. Even so, Kyle stood taller than she.

Movement came from the left, and she turned her head to see a large, tan feline with a white belly sprinting toward them. The puma began changing its shape but didn't stop running. As it drew near, it became more human with each step. He stopped a couple feet away, completely naked. The man glanced between Kyle and her.

Rubia kept her gaze from dipping below the sleek man's bronze waist. Just barely, though. She refused to become interested in these men who shapeshifted with such ease.

"Kyle, the men—" the werepuma said, slightly out of breath.

Kyle growled a low rumbling sound and nodded to the side, away from Rubia. The man bowed his head and stalked away from them to wait. Kyle turned his attention back to her. "We're not done. I'll see you later."

She held his stare and remained silent.

He turned away and moved at speeds faster than her eyes could follow.

Probably to intimidate, or even impress her. Well, it hadn't worked. She wouldn't allow herself to be easily charmed.

* * *

Kyle stopped running once he was well away from the tall, gorgeous Amazon who constantly disregarded him. His jaw clenched, and he turned to face his second in command. The way she'd only just kept her curious gaze from taking in the other man's body made jealousy surge through him. Who was he becoming? This wasn't like him.

He sucked in a breath and let it out slowly. "What do you want, Jorge? What about the men?"

"We were concerned. You didn't tell us about your departure." Jorge lowered his head slightly, which was a customary greeting for their kind when talking with the leader. Kyle had done the same with his predecessor, who had fallen during the attack on the Amazon's camp. The former leader had let jealousy rage through him when Rei mating with the Amazon princess, claiming her as his own. Why the leader had thought he had a chance with Adara, Kyle had no clue.

Kyle shook the thought from his head. He hadn't understood the man's motive then, and he couldn't fully grasp it now. "What troubles the camp? Why did you seek me out?"

"You called together a meeting that's to begin soon." Jorge glanced over his shoulder toward the direction of their camp before looking back at Kyle.

"Right. I guess I got a little distracted." How foolish. Did Rubia really have that kind of hold on him? He grimaced.

Jorge's lips curved in a grin, and he clasped a hand on Kyle's shoulder. "With a fine woman like that, there's little wonder. Any man would feel the same."

Kyle narrowed his eyes at the comment and barely restrained his beast from growling. But Jorge was one of the werepumas he knew was loyal to him. Others had accepted his right to rule after the death of the old leader, but the rumors he'd heard around camp told him he wouldn't have been their prime choice.

They weren't thrilled about an outsider ruling over them. Nevertheless, they'd have to learn to respect him since he wasn't going anywhere. Not away from the Pride, his position, or this land. Besides, he'd arranged peace between themselves and the Amazons, not an easy task since the warrior women kept very much to themselves.

Then again, his connection to Rei had probably helped more than he wanted to admit.

Kyle strode forward, breaking away from Jorge's amiable grip. His thoughts turned back to the way Rubia felt beneath him. To her wide eyes staring up at him as the scent of her arousal teased his nose. He forced away the memory. "We should head back. The meeting waits."

Jorge matched his stride. "Good, good. What will you talk about today?"

"I'm going to address the people about the recent rumors." Simple as that. He'd give them a piece of his mind. Everyone needed to get on the same page.

Jorge stopped suddenly and cleared his throat. "What? Are you sure you should do something like that? We're not entirely sure about the position of some members of the camp. You shouldn't put yourself in danger like this. The people don't need yet another leader dead in such a short period of time. The Pride needs someone who will last."

"Which is exactly why I'm doing this. I don't plan on going anywhere." Kyle gave Jorge a small smile. "Trust me, okay?"

Jorge's frown deepened a second before it disappeared. "Right. I trust you."

2

Rubia walked through the village gates and glanced at the queen's throne. Adara sat with her belly ever more swollen. Rei crouched at her feet on the steps leading to the platform. They were talking and laughing together, the way she used to with Rubia.

Rubia sighed and turned away, only to see the Wise Woman walking in her direction. Maybe she was on her way to visit someone else. It wasn't often the Wise Woman sought her out. Rubia held back a frown and did her best to keep a neutral face.

The Wise Woman's eyes sparkled with knowledge and magic in her well-worn, wrinkled face. "Rubia, it's been a while since we talked. Did you have a nice rest in your hammock?"

Rubia blinked and cocked her head to the side. She hadn't told anyone about her hammock or that she was heading out. "It was fine." Aside from a bruised bum.

"You experienced more than you were expecting. Come, I'll give you something for your sore back."

"I'm fine really. It's just a bump." What she wanted was a nap. She'd done her chores for the morning, and she'd continue with her work later in the afternoon.

"No, I insist, child. I have news for you." She smiled and took Rubia by the elbow. "Come now."

Rubia's jaw dropped. News? What kind of news would the Wise Woman have for her? She wasn't like Adara, who received news, as had her mother, for the good of their tribe.

Glancing at the throne again, Rubia saw her queen spot her. Adara smiled and raised her hand. Beside her, Rei's gaze followed Adara's, and he waved to her as well. Rubia returned the gesture. Wow, they'd noticed her.

"They haven't forgotten about you," the Wise Woman said, drawing her attention. "Adara has experienced quite a bit of late."

Rubia frowned. The Wise Woman was right. Her childhood friend did have a lot going on. Finding her mate, leading an attack on enemies, becoming their queen, finding peace with the werepumas, and now her pregnancy. Maybe Rubia didn't give Adara as much credit as she should.

"Here we are." The Wise Woman released her grip on Rubia and opened the door to her hut. A bedroll lay in one corner in the small room. On the other wall was a table with various plants and tools neatly laid out. Another smaller, simpler table sat to one side for eating, with an ornate woven rug underneath it. From the stories Rubia had heard, the rug had belonged to the village's wise women for generations before her.

Rubia hadn't been here for a while. It wasn't much different from her own home, aside from the area where the Wise Woman worked on her herbal concoctions. Rubia leaned her spear against the wall and stood to one side of the room. The Wise Woman's healing ways weren't unknown to her. She'd been under her careful attention before.

Rubia crossed the distance to the bed and lay on her stomach. "What news do you have for me?"

The Wise Woman smiled and crushed a few herbs in a small bowl on the table. "You will become a woman soon, as Adara has. The Indian men will arrive within a few days." Her voice was neutral and pleasant.

Rubia blinked and turned her gaze away. She wasn't sure how she felt about the responsibility she'd known would eventually come. Soon, her time would come when she'd do her duty to the tribe and lay with a man. Hopefully she would conceive a daughter. She'd raise her young and do her part to keep the village going as her mother and grandmother before her.

Yet from the mysterious twinkle in the Wise Woman's eye, Rubia couldn't help but wonder if there was more to the news than she let on. Rubia refused to push for information, especially from an elder.

The Wise Woman came to her side and rubbed a healing ointment over her back on the spot that hurt the most.

Rubia clenched her jaw to keep from voicing her pain. After a few moments, the pain lessened to an ache. How could the Wise Woman heal so quickly with her herbal remedies? It always astounded Rubia.

"There you go, child. If you feel any more pain, you're welcome to come by my home again." The Wise Woman patted her on the shoulder and returned the bowl of ointment to the table.

Rubia climbed to her feet and nodded to the older woman. "Thank you."

"You are most welcome. Take care, and do not push yourself too hard. Be in good condition when the time of your womanhood comes." She turned her back and took a few different herbs from the worktable.

Rubia retrieved her spear and left the small hut. She sighed and walked home. Before she could get inside, she heard her name being called.

Adara strode toward her with Rei at her side. He rarely left her side these days. Not a surprise considering her current condition. "How are you doing, my friend?" she asked.

Rubia saluted with her spear in the way of their traditions. "I'm fine. Thank you, my queen."

Adara glanced around at the others nearby doing the same thing. She nodded toward Rubia's home.

Once inside, she frowned. "Are you sure you're okay?" She plucked a few dried leaves from Rubia's hair. "It looks like you were in a fight."

"Nothing major. The Wise Woman has healed me." She set her spear aside and sat at her dining table on one of the low seats.

"The Wise Woman also told you about the Indian males coming soon, I presume?" Adara asked, lowering herself next to her.

"Yes. She did." Rubia picked out the rest of the leaves from her hair, annoyed she'd been walking around the village like this. Now everyone probably thought her to be out getting into trouble or, worse yet, that she was clumsy. She fought to keep the grimace from her face.

"You know once you have lain with a man you won't be able to find another unless the one you're with dies, yes?" Adara watched her carefully, as if that were supposed to mean something.

"I've gone through the Wise Woman's talk the same as you. What are you trying to say?" Rubia rubbed her slightly sweaty palms over the cloth covering her hips.

Rei cleared his throat, bringing her attention to him. "If you're interested in Kyle, you need to let it be known before time runs out."

Rubia's jaw slackened, and she stared at Rei before swiveling her gaze to Adara. Had they come to her home to talk to her about the werepuma leader? She closed her mouth and frowned. "Thank you for your concern, but I'm fully capable of reaching that conclusion myself. I'll make sure to tell the Wise Woman if the need arises." She walked to her bed and sat on the edge. "For now, I need some rest as instructed by our elder. If you'll excuse me."

Adara and Rei exchanged an uneasy look.

"Yes, of course. You know where to find me if you ever want to talk." Adara opened the door to Rubia's hut and stepped outside.

Rei lingered in the doorway and glanced back at Rubia. "You should give the man a chance. And I'm sure Adara would like it if you…" He paused and shook his head.

"If I what?"

"If you didn't hide yourself away so often. She misses your friendship." He gave her a quick nod and left before she could say anything in return.

Rubia's jaw dropped, and she placed her face in her hands. That kicked her in the gut. Had she not done what she could? Was it her fault their friendship seemed to be on rocky ground?

* * *

Kyle crossed his arms over his chest and paced in front of his werepumas. He held his shoulders back and his chin up, trying to display confidence and leadership. The chink Rubia had created in his hard exterior made that difficult. That she held such sway over him made him yearn to work harder at making her want him too.

But maybe he needed to give her time. That's what he had on his hands these days, right? Lots of time.

Jorge was seated to one side of the gathered men, his legs crossed at the ankle as he watched Kyle. A small frown creased his brow and brought Kyle back to the moment.

"I am going to be very clear with everyone here. We might have differing opinions about who should be in charge of this Pride, but one thing we absolutely need is mutual respect."

A soft murmur rose from the group of men.

"If we don't respect each other, this group will not have a constant leader. Uprisings will happen, and then the Pride will be thrown into finding another werepuma who is strong enough to watch over all of you." Kyle stopped and stared pointedly at the men who he'd heard had wanted to overthrow him.

They dropped their gazes in submission, and a small boost of victory coursed through him. At least they weren't so proud as to cause him problems at the moment. If they'd had the support behind them, there was the chance they would have moved on him then. Something in his favor.

Jorge gave a subtle nod and smiled. He'd been a strong member of this Pride for several years, whereas Kyle was a fairly recent addition. The sole reason they'd taken Kyle in was one of their members had attacked him when he'd been out with Rei observing different species of animals and some plants as a biologist.

He hadn't been aware of Rei's weretiger side before his transformation into a werepuma. They'd fallen out of touch because Rei blamed himself for the attack, and yet Kyle had felt more alive than ever.

But what made Kyle their current leader was his power. He'd come to terms with who he was, and the group respected him for his quick acceptance. Although, some more than others.

"Does anyone have anything to say about this?" Kyle asked.

"You brought us together for a meeting about this?" Eduardo said. "Or was there something else you wanted to mention as well?"

Kyle raised an eyebrow. It was hard to say where Eduardo's loyalty rested. "This is important to discuss. I'm the leader of the Pride, and I want to make sure everyone understands each other. If you have something you want to say, let's hear it."

"Are you going soft on that girl? Our old leader lost focus because of a girl, and look at where that got him. Dead." Eduardo's lips curled, and a soft trickle of a growl escaped his lips.

Kyle roared and took a step toward the crowd, only to have Jorge step between him and his people, namely Eduardo. "I am not like the old leader. I was the one who made peace with the Amazon tribe after the disturbance he caused. And I have not gone soft." He glanced around at the other tribesmen. "Would you say the few others who have mated with Amazon women have gone soft? Do you dare?"

Eduardo's nostrils flared, and he shook his head in a quick jerk. "No, for they have claimed their mate and will build the numbers of the two camps. What can be said about your attempts?"

Kyle's blood boiled at the insult. Eduardo said what he'd been feeling, but the mention in front of his entire Pride stung. "You don't have a place to talk seeing as how you have not even tried to form a relationship with one of the women." Kyle crossed his arms over his chest and narrowed his eyes, keeping his gaze directly on Eduardo's in a show of dominance. Not something he cared for, but he would not tolerate someone ripping into him in front of his people.

Eduardo's jaw clenched, and he lowered his gaze before stalking off. A few feet away from the group, he took his puma form, then raced into the forest.

"This meeting is finished, unless anyone else has something to say." Kyle stared at the group, daring them to speak. He desired a fight at the moment.

No one spoke. They all sat or stood quietly.

Kyle nodded and walked toward his tent. He wanted to be alone. He'd see Rubia again later as he'd said, but for now, he couldn't stand the sight of another human.

3

The setting sun created brilliant colors as twilight and evening neared. Rubia's tribeswomen cooked food over the fire pit near the center of the village, preparing for a night of storytelling and community.

Rubia sat to one side of the fire, a little away from everyone else, and leaned back, looking up through the trees at the sky. A small part of her wondered what Kyle was doing since he'd promised to see her later, but that didn't matter. She didn't want his company, right?

Thoughts of him made her wonder about Adara and Rei. They'd mentioned she would be tied to one man, and if she were to couple with an Indian, Kyle would be off-limits to her. Why would Adara and Rei be interested in who she mated with? Had Kyle mentioned something to them?

Her gaze sought them, and she flinched when she noticed Adara and Rei walking across the open area toward the fire. After what happened earlier, she didn't know if she could handle being near them. Her pride hurt, and yet she knew then she'd been wrong.

Rubia stood, determined to make things right with her childhood friend. A strong hand touched her shoulder. She swirled around to see Kyle in front of her. His face looked grim and hard.

"I didn't mean to startle you," he said, dropping his hand to his side.

"It's fine. I didn't hear you approach. Maybe next time you can make a little more noise." Her pulse slowed gradually, and she propped a hand on her hip.

His lip tugged up at the corner, and mirth sparkled in his eyes. "You want me to stomp around your village, so you can hear me?"

The way his eyes gleamed captivated her, and she tore her gaze from his. His words made her feel like she'd been silly with her request. "Well, if you

51

put it that way…" She shook her head. "No, disregard what I said." She glanced over her shoulder at Adara and Rei, both of whom watched her and Kyle while talking amongst themselves.

A sting of self-awareness hit her, and she forced a smile. She raised a hand to wave at them, and they returned the gesture.

"If you'd like to go to them, don't let me stop you." Kyle's voice drew her attention back to him. The laughter had faded from his features, and he stared at her intently. His gaze swept over her body before swiftly returning to her face.

Frustration built within her, and she wanted nothing more than to flee from her village and run through the mighty rainforest, but that would gain her nothing. She needed to stand firm and deal with things. That was all she could do.

And the first thing she needed to handle was what she'd do about Kyle. She wanted to tell him to find someone else since he wore down her defenses, but something within her wouldn't allow that.

The Wise Woman had said within a few days Rubia would have her womanhood as Adara had. So that meant from the Indians, right? Yet there was something in the way she'd stated it. Adara hadn't become a woman by an Indian.

Rubia crossed her arms over her chest and stared at Kyle. "What do you want? Why have you taken such an interest in me?"

He glanced around at the tribeswomen milling around them. "If you don't mind, I'd rather discuss this somewhere private."

She frowned and watched the interest in the eye of her neighbor as Sol walked by on the way toward the food. "Fine. Let's go to my hut for a moment then." She didn't really want to have him in her home, but if he was going to give her the answers she desired, then she needed to allow him.

They crossed the village to her hut, and she opened the door, letting him inside. She closed the door and turned to face him.

His gaze wandered around his surroundings.

She suppressed a grimace and wondered what his camp was like, or even what his home had been like before he'd come to her homeland. Probably better than her hut, but this was the only home she'd known. Frustration built within her at the way he made her feel and the fact she second-guessed herself.

His expression remained the same as he looked at her. Neutral, interested, and maybe curious?

Self-awareness washed over her, and she shrugged it away. Her teeth bit into her lower lip, only to have his gaze dip to watch. She immediately stopped and waved to her dining table. "Shall we?"

He shrugged his tense shoulders. "I'm fine here. You wanted me to answer your questions, right? I don't think I need to sit for that." He ran his hand through his hair. "Thanks for the offer."

"If you insist." She remained standing as well, following his lead.

Kyle stayed silent for a moment and then let out a breath. He returned to glancing at her hut. "I'm sorry if I've come across as rude. I haven't had a very good day. I'm under some pressure with my group." He balled his hands into fists once, twice, then seemed to forcefully relax.

"It's fine. Answer my questions. I need to get back to the fire before my people become curious about what you're doing with me in here. This isn't appropriate, you know." She'd already had people suspect there was something between the two of them.

He gave a sharp nod. "What do I want? Rubia, I want you. Why am I interested in you? You make me feel things I haven't thought to want in a long time. Desire. Passion." He shrugged and waved his hands in the air. "I can't help myself. I've felt this way since I first met you. You fill something that was lost inside me."

She frowned and sat on one of the chairs, not knowing what to say to that. How could she have stirred up emotions in him when she'd done nothing to encourage him? She barely understood what was going on. Why would he want to open up to her like this? And really, what was she going to do? She was more confused than ever.

In a few days, she'd come fully into womanhood, and yet now Kyle had expressed his interest in her verbally. His behavior toward her, which she'd disregarded as him being friendly or annoying, was now apparent. He'd kissed her and pursued her because he wanted her.

How was she supposed to react to this?

Blinking, she looked at him.

His eyes tightened, and he seemed to implore her to give a reaction, but she froze. Emotions between a man and woman were uncharted territory to her.

After a moment, his lips thinned into a pink line, and he lowered his gaze. "Do you have nothing to say?" His hands started to ball into fists again, but he stopped himself.

"I'm at a loss for words." She wanted to go to him. Place her hand against his shoulder. Do something, but she couldn't move. She couldn't fathom what to do.

"I see." He took a step toward the door of her hut.

"I..." She wondered if she should tell him of the upcoming ceremony she'd have with the Indians soon, but surely he wouldn't want to know this.

He glanced over his shoulder at her and waited.

She shook her head.

Kyle walked to the door and placed his hand against it.

"Wait, are you going to stick around for the storytelling and food?" she asked, rising to her feet. Part of her didn't want him to go, especially not with the sting of hurt in his eyes.

He stayed still and silent. She wondered if he'd respond to her question or just keep standing there. He released the door and turned to face her. "Should I?"

"If you don't have other plans, that is." She smiled, trying to break the awkward vibe radiating through the atmosphere.

"Okay then. I'll stay for a little while." He stepped toward her and brushed his knuckles across her cheek. Tenderness flowed through that gesture. Something she'd rarely experienced before.

She enjoyed the feeling of his strong touch, but why should she get caught up in something she wouldn't be able to keep? She and Kyle were too different to work well together, weren't they? Besides, his responsibility was to his werepumas, and she had hers to her people. And yet, that felt like a half-hearted excuse.

He moved closer, and she stood her ground. She wouldn't flee from him. Not anymore. She'd made that decision. She'd face what frightened her.

Kyle's hand trailed down her jaw and then dipped lower to her neck and to her shoulder. The sensations rushing through her were pleasant. Warmth heated her body, making the already warm night even hotter. He brought his hand back up and caressed his thumb over her cheek, very close to her lips.

She closed her eyes at the nice feeling roiling through her. Hot breath trailed across her chin a moment before soft lips met hers. She peeked her eyes open to see Kyle very near her with his eyes closed. She shut her eyes again, letting herself get carried away.

He placed his hand on her waist and pulled her body to his. She placed her hands against his chest, and hard muscles flexed under her touch. Memories of when they'd been together in her hammock earlier stirred in her mind.

A wet touch of the tip of his tongue met her lips, and she pulled away. His gaze was slightly dazed, and heat burned in his eyes.

She wiped away a drop of sweat from her forehead and sucked in a breath. "What are you doing to me?" she said. Her voice cracked, and she cleared her throat.

"I... I'm sorry. I went too far." He ran his hands through his hair and turned away, resting his hand against the wall of her hut.

"It's okay. I'm just not... used to this kind of thing. These sensations... emotions are new to me." She sat at her table again and placed her forehead against the solid wood. Her body tingled with desire and heat. She'd definitely need a moment to regain her composure before seeing her fellow villagers. The things Kyle had done... she almost wished to continue.

Should she even be having those kinds of feelings, though? She looked back at him. He had straightened but was still breathing in and out in a controlled manner. Maybe their intimacy had affected him as much as it had her. Perhaps, if not more so.

He nodded. "I understand. I just don't want to take advantage of you, unless you want me to." He turned, and his gaze pinned her in place.

Warmth built within her, and she wanted to feel the strangely pleasant sensations he'd stirred within her again. Outside, the evening's festivities were beginning.

Kyle's gaze flicked to her door, and his jaw clenched. "You should head back before anyone gets suspicious."

"You're going as well, right?" She raised an eyebrow at him.

He stared at her pointedly. "I'm not sure that would be a good idea."

She shot to her feet. "Why? Tired of me already?" Her nostrils flared, and she shook her head, stomping to the door of her hut. "That doesn't matter. Within a few days, I shall become a woman, and you won't be able to toy with me so."

* * *

Kyle's jaw clenched with the first stirring of anger. How could she be so callous about what they'd just shared? Maybe he shouldn't have tried to distance himself, but she affected him more than anyone he'd met before. And he'd had his share of women before.

Her words finally struck him. He cocked his head to the side, unable to fathom what she was talking about. She'd soon be coming into her womanhood? He wouldn't be able to toy with her then? What was that supposed to mean?

She stood there, spine straight, as if daring him to do something.

He wouldn't because he valued her. Part of him wanted to ask what the heck she meant, but the other half of him just wanted to run away from her village as a puma, savoring the speed and senses of his feline beast.

Rubia shrugged a shoulder and walked out, closing the door behind her. The sound of her retreating footsteps from outside couldn't muffle the sharp sigh he heard her release, and he almost wished he'd stopped her.

A soft knock came from the door, and he frowned. Who could that be? Her people were all out at the bonfire enjoying the evening.

He took a deep breath and smelled a familiar scent. Rei.

"Come in," Kyle called out.

The door opened, and the tall Russian stood in the doorway. "I'm guessing things did not go so well?"

Kyle grimaced and nodded. "Yeah, you can say that again." He sat at Rubia's table and ran his fingers over the wooden surface. "I don't know how to reach her. She's different."

"We've noticed as well. She's not been her usual self." Rei strode to the other side of the table and seated himself too.

"I'm not sure what I'm doing wrong. I'm okay with women, but she's just something else." Maybe Rei would be the perfect person to confide in, since he'd surely gone through some of the same trials with Adara. They'd been mated now for some months. He looked at them and saw what he wanted for himself. Something he wanted with Rubia, if only she'd let him in.

Rei nodded. "That's the thing with trying to mate with an Amazon. You have to throw out some of what you'd expect from other women. It takes patience connecting with them."

"I'm not sure if I have time for a lot of patience. She mentioned something about how she'd soon become a woman. What is that supposed to mean?" He looked at Rei askance, hoping his friend would know what was going on.

Rei's pleasant demeanor faltered, and his lips fell into a frown. "Right. Well, the Amazon women obviously have to reproduce to keep their numbers up, so they made a kind of agreement with the local Indians to copulate." He looked increasingly uncomfortable with the subject. "Once the Amazon has come into womanhood through those means, she's untouchable by other men. So if Rubia were to… have sex with an Indian, she'd be out of your reach." He met Kyle's gaze. "I'm sorry to be the one to break that to you."

Kyle gritted his teeth and balled his hands into fists. Why had he kissed her? Why had she allowed him to show that kind of intimacy with her if she knew he didn't have a chance? Were her people so primitive she had no idea what those things meant? She couldn't even tell him not to waste his time with her? "It's fine. I'm glad you told me."

Rei frowned at him. "You really do care about her, don't you?"

Kyle didn't know what to say, but he nodded. Part of him burned for her, and the other wondered if he shouldn't just let her go.

"Don't give up, if she's what you want." Rei leaned back and gave him a nod of confidence. Like he had full faith the situation would resolve itself.

"I'll have to think about this. It's a lot to take in." He stood, needing to get out of this Amazon village. He felt so alone for the first time in a while. Not only were his werepumas grumbling behind his back, but the woman he cared about would soon be out of his grasp forever if he couldn't convince her to mate with him. He wished luck, or even fate, were on his side. "You had things easy, friend." He huffed and forced a smile.

"Seems so. She'll come around." Rei rose to his feet and patted Kyle on the shoulder.

"Perhaps."

"You're welcome to join Adara and me at the campfire. We'd enjoy having your company." Rei headed to the door of Rubia's hut.

"Thank you for the offer, but I'm heading back to my camp. I've had enough interaction with others for the day. No offense." He followed Rei outside and closed the door behind him.

"None taken. You'll have to stop by and visit sometime soon." Rei held out his hand, and they clasped forearms.

"Sure thing. Have a nice evening." He slunk into the shadows. His gaze caught on Rubia before he had the chance to leave. She sat alone to one side of the fire and held herself differently than normal. As if she were distraught.

Someone walked by her, and she waved away their concerns. Soon, she stood and walked toward the village's gates, slipping out. She didn't have her spear with her. Perhaps he should follow. He wouldn't want to see her hurt.

No, she was an Amazon. She'd be fine.

4

Rubia walked into the forest and headed toward her hammock. It was nighttime, and she knew the dangers of going away during the night, but she wanted space from the laughter and happiness radiating from the campfire. She wanted to be able to think about the encounter she'd had with Kyle. It still confused her, and she wished he'd opened up to her instead of shutting down. He confused her, and she didn't like feeling those feelings. She'd had clarity in her life before Adara had mated with Rei, but especially before the werepumas had decided to ally with her people, and Kyle had decided... What had he decided? He wanted her. Good for him.

She didn't know how to handle that. She'd enjoyed his kisses, but... Geez... She didn't know what she wanted, but maybe she wanted him.

He brought up feelings within her, stroking her cheek and making her feel. How could anyone compare with that? How could she go back to whatever would come with the Indians? They'd arrive, do what was required between a man and woman, and then leave until they were next required. She didn't see that as any way to be. Adara and Rei seemed so happy together.

She climbed into the hammock and sighed. Staring into the trees, she wrapped her arms around herself. Peace and tranquility that hadn't been there before started to soak into her. She closed her eyes and let herself smile.

Moments passed and unease came over her, as if she was being watched. Could it be one of her people checking to make sure she was okay?

She glanced in the direction of her village but saw no one. She continued to scan the forest around her, and again nobody was in view. Worry chased over her skin, and she pushed to her feet. Her safety relied on getting back to the village. She didn't like the vibes going through the air. Danger lurked in the shadows. And if she didn't move fast enough, it would close in and encompass her.

She ran toward her village, but a large, dark figure blocked her way. She slid to a stop and headed another direction, only to be stopped by another dark figure. Glancing the opposite way, she noticed she was being surrounded. Who in their right mind would get this close to her village? Besides, the only people who knew about her village were the Indians and the... werepumas.

Fear choked her. Could Kyle have put them up to this? Was he striking out at her because of their negative encounter? She straightened her spine and crossed her arms over her chest. No, she wouldn't cower to him or his people.

"What do you want?" she asked, wanting only to reach her kinsfolk.

None of the figures around her replied. Instead they slowly, methodically, closed in on her position.

She dropped into a fighting stance, ready to take them on with her bare hands. She wouldn't let them think she was easy prey. Not at all.

Movement in the distance drew her attention. The shadow behind her grabbed her, slapping his hand over her mouth.

She shot her elbow back into his ribs. He made a loud oomph. She kicked her legs, trying to strike him, but he seemed unaffected by her effort.

Instead, his fingertips pushed brutally into her neck. Her body weakened, and the world turned dark. She could only feel the dim sensation of being lifted over the person's shoulder and carried off at a quick pace.

* * *

Kyle walked toward Rubia's hammock anyway. He needed to know she was okay out in the rainforest alone. He wouldn't make himself known to her, just watch her from a distance.

Why he'd do that he wasn't sure, since part of him felt betrayed, but he couldn't blame her for it all. He'd had his own part to play in what had happened between them in her hut.

The moment he drew near enough, he knew something wasn't right. He heard the soft noise of struggle and sensed movement. By the time he reached her hammock, she wasn't there. He ran his hand through his hair and then shook his head. Who the hell would do this?

He sniffed the air and smelled the familiar scent of werepuma. Dread filled him, and he couldn't believe he'd been so stupid. He'd shown weakness in wanting Rubia, and now they were using her against him. His people were trying to take her from him.

He crouched and looked around at the ground in hopes of seeing some sign of which direction they'd gone. Not finding much—since he didn't have the skills of a tracker—he pulled off his clothes and set them in Rubia's hammock, then shifted into his puma form. He'd have enhanced senses, which would make it easier to find where she'd been taken. And most importantly, he'd be able to get her back that much quicker.

He ran through the rainforest. His senses guided him until he caught the sound of leaves crunching ahead. That had to be them. Moving closer to the location, he noticed Rubia slumped on the ground. Four men stood around her. He couldn't see their faces very well, but he knew they were werepumas from his Pride.

Someone would be paying with his life for this grievance against him and against Rubia. He slid into his werepuma form that was half-human, half-puma and watched the men from behind a tree, staying cloaked in the shadows. Although he didn't plan on hiding very long. Soon enough, they'd figure out he was here, anyway. And soon enough, he'd exact his justice.

One of the men went to Rubia. He grabbed her by her long, brown hair and pulled her head up at an awkward angle. He muttered something in Portuguese that Kyle couldn't quite catch and dropped her back to the ground.

His lips curled back from his teeth with menace, and he stalked closer to the men and Rubia, unable to leash the beast within him that craved blood for the assault against the one he desired as mate. The female who called to the savage part of him and soothed it.

He rumbled low in his chest, and all heads turned to him. A too-familiar scent hit his nose at the same time the man faced him. Kyle froze in his steps. How could Jorge do this?

He leapt at Jorge and landed on the ground when his second in command deftly dodged the attack. He turned and growled, swatting a large paw at one of the men who closed in on him. "Why have you done this?" he roared.

"You've shown weakness," Jorge said. "I don't approve of you constantly fawning over this woman. Your Pride should hold more importance to you than she does." He held his ground, standing tall in his human form. He wouldn't have enough time to shift before Kyle could rip his throat out. Being in the middle of a shift left one vulnerable to attack. They both knew that.

He watched Jorge and kept himself open, allowing his focus to stay alert so he'd be able to tell if they would attack. One against four wasn't good odds, but he was strong. And they were in human form.

One of the men to his side began to shift. Kyle dove for him. The one at his back lunged, and Kyle ducked so the man hit the werepuma in front of him. Kyle grabbed the big cat, and clutched his throat, squeezing until bones cracked beneath his grip. That wouldn't kill the cat, but he'd take a long time to heal.

The third guy ran at him, and Kyle swiped his massive paw at him, slicing open his belly. The bulge of shiny intestines peeked out, and the traitor screamed, pressing his hands against his stomach.

Someone jumped on his back. A knife blade stabbed into him, and pain ripped through him. Hissing, he rammws backwards into a nearby tree. A whoosh of air heaved from the man behind him. Kyle slammed into the tree again for good measure, and the man fell off.

Kyle plucked the knife from his back and tossed it in the air, assessing the blade before turning his gaze to Jorge. "I'm not weak. You're greedy and jealous of my rise to power. If you're so confident you can overcome me in battle, you should try." He heard rustling from behind him and threw the knife. Glancing over his shoulder, he noticed the blade stuck in the other werepuma's chest. He returned his focus to Jorge. He didn't like killing his men. They were already weakened from the previous attack when some of them had fought against the Amazon women.

Rubia lay on the ground behind Jorge. Her eyes were closed, but her breathing appeared steady. "Step away from the girl, and I will not hurt you, even if you have been traitorous to me." Baring his teeth, he took a step forward, but he stayed silent, trying not to overtly threaten Jorge. He didn't want the other man to act too irrationally.

"You won't hurt me? You've killed members of our pride."

"And that was *your* fault." Kyle snarled, and the sound of it filled the air around them, leaving the forest quiet in the aftermath.

"But who will people believe? They'll believe me, since I am the stable advisor, whereas you are not capable of leading." He smiled confidently and turned toward Rubia.

Kyle launched himself through the air, slamming them both into a tree. Jorge punched Kyle in the ribs. His supernatural strength even in human form surprised Kyle, and he fell away from the traitor. But Kyle quickly gained his feet again and watched him, making sure he didn't escape or go near Rubia. He would not allow her to be harmed.

Footsteps sounded in the distance, and he knew from the soft rattle of equipment that the Amazons were on the way. Maybe they'd noticed Rubia gone or heard Kyle's anger.

Jorge didn't seem to hear the approaching female warriors at first, but then panic flew over his face. He leapt to his feet and started to run, but Kyle tackled him to the ground, holding his teeth over the other man's throat. He didn't want to harm him. He just wanted to make sure Jorge didn't take off before justice could be dealt. The Amazons would probably want their part in punishing these men for taking one of their tribeswomen, and he surely knew he wanted to deal with them after they'd intended to harm the one he cared about. He grimaced and bit a little harder at the thought. The coppery taste of blood trickled into his mouth, and Jorge squirmed beneath him. Adrenaline and fear flowed through Jorge's blood, making it taste all the sweeter to Kyle.

The animal side of him perked up, unable to resist, and he growled, giving in to animal instinct.

Jorge's eyes widened, and he bucked, shoving at the wall of Kyle's chest.

Kyle would not be moved. He would not let his inner beast get the best of him. He would resist. He had to. He couldn't let Jorge win the sympathy of the Pride. His Pride.

He looked over and saw Rubia move slowly to a sitting position. Her gaze shifted to a point behind him, out of his range of vision, but he held his focus on her, letting her presence soothe his wild beast.

Rei walked in front of Kyle. "Kyle? Rubia? What's going on?"

Rubia started to stand, but she fell back to the earth. "I... the men grabbed me. Did something to my neck." Her hand went to her neck, and she winced in pain. "I passed out, and now I'm here." Emotion shimmered on her face. "Kyle saved me."

He wanted to drop everything, go to her and comfort her. Hold her in his arms and make everything right. Make her feel what he felt for her alone.

"Kyle," Rei said. "Let go of him. I'll make sure he doesn't go anywhere. We need to know what's going on. We can help."

Movement sounded around him, and he glanced to see Amazons surrounding him. The tall, blonde woman he'd noticed earlier helped Rubia stand. He reluctantly released Jorge and hovered over him. He'd make sure the bastard didn't get away until Rei had a solid grip on him.

Once Rei secured Jorge, Kyle stepped away. He sat and huffed out a puff of air. "He took her while she was walking out by herself. Him and the others." His voice sounded gravelly and rough to his own ears. Inhuman. Which shouldn't surprise anyone, since he was in his werepuma form. "They must've knocked her out. I followed and confronted them. They attacked me, so I fought back. To protect her."

"Weak," Jorge said, a hiss of sound.

Rei punched Jorge in the jaw, knocking him out cold. "Don't listen to him. You did a noble thing, and the Amazons appreciate you looking after Rubia." Rei's eyes said he figured there was more to the story, but he was letting that rest for now while the Amazons were in earshot.

Kyle turned his gaze back to Rubia, and she nodded. "Thank you, Kyle." A blush ran up her cheeks, apparent to him in the night due to his heightened vision.

She stumbled on a rock, and the Amazon holding her struggled to regain her grip. It looked like this woman wasn't used to fighting much.

Kyle willed his body into human form. He wanted to help Rubia back to the village. Her eyes widened, and she watched in shock as his bones cracked and muscles ripped apart and reshaped. Pain seared him as he went through the shift. He sucked in a deep breath and let it out slowly from his human shape.

The Amazons around him each stood their ground, but their eyes widened slightly. The look of amazement and a small amount of fear glimmered in their gazes before, one by one, they could shut down their emotions. All except Rubia. She stared at him, the whites in her eyes visible. Her jaw was slack, and she blinked after a moment.

He crossed the space between them and wrapped his arm around her, touching the warm, bare skin of her waist. He wanted to rub his hands all over her and bury himself within her.

Rubia put her hand on his waist and walked through the rainforest beside him. The woman on her other side stole a glance at him, obviously trying to see what a naked male body looked like. A slight smile curved her lips, and a look of wonder passed over her face before she averted her gaze.

Rubia kept her head slightly down as they trekked back to the village. Around them, the other Amazons carried the injured or dead werepumas. Rei held Jorge over his shoulder.

Kyle glanced at Rubia again, enjoying being so close without her scrambling to get away. He could get used to this.

5

Hyperawareness filled Rubia at Kyle being so close. His hand on her bare skin tantalized and sent small shivers through her, but she held herself still and tried not to give in to the gentle persuasion to melt in his strong arms.

At her side, she noticed Sol checking out Kyle, and a twinge of jealousy reared its head within her.

Jealousy?

She couldn't believe it, and yet that was what it was. She wanted him. What he'd done for her... She wanted to thank him in the one way she could. Becoming his mate was something she'd warred with, and she still didn't fully understand everything involved. But if Adara and Rei were so happy, she knew happiness would be possible for her and Kyle. It had to be.

But what if Kyle didn't want her anymore? After what she'd said and done? Worry bubbled up, but she shoved it down. She could think of that later when they were able to talk freely.

After a few moments, they reached the village. A couple other werepumas were there, looking concerned. A tall, dark-haired man frowned and walked closer to them.

"Eduardo, what are you doing here?" Kyle asked, coming to a stop and forcing her and Sol to do the same.

"The Amazons told us what happened. We wanted to come and make sure everything was okay." He bowed his head. "I may not fully agree with you, but I accept you as my leader."

"Thank you," Kyle said, holding out his arm.

Eduardo clasped Kyle's forearm. "You're welcome. Is there anything I can do?"

Kyle glanced over his shoulder, and Rubia tried to as well but her neck hurt too much. "There is one dead and a few wounded. If you could help the Amazons with them, I would appreciate it." He sighed, hanging his head slightly. "I didn't want to do it."

"I understand. I'll go help and report to you about their conditions later." Eduardo nodded and walked off, following the sound of pained moans.

"Let's get you to your hut to rest. Perhaps your friend—" Kyle began.

"My name is Sol," her neighbor supplied.

Kyle smiled and inclined his head. "Perhaps Sol could fetch the Wise Woman to take a look at you."

"It would be my pleasure." She eased away from Rubia gently.

"Thank you," Rubia said, her voice a little scratchy.

Sol smiled and sprinted off toward the Wise Woman's home. The door to the her hut opened just before Sol reached it.

Kyle continued walking, and she held him a little tighter even if her head was now clearing. She almost didn't want the Wise Woman's attention quite yet, but she glanced over her shoulder to see the older woman heading toward her home. A mysterious smile spread across the Wise Woman's lips.

Kyle opened the door to her home and helped her inside the narrow doorway. "Let's get you settled on the bed," he said, his voice husky and rough. He walked her over to the bed and helped her into a comfortable position, then covered her with the well-worn blanket her grandmother had made years ago.

She looked up at him, and he knelt on the floor next to the bed.

"I'm glad you're safe," he said.

"It's thanks to you. I shouldn't have walked off like that."

"No, you shouldn't have, but they should not have taken or hurt you either." He sighed.

He brushed away a strand of hair from her face. His shoulders tensed, and he tilted his head to the side, glancing at the door. Suddenly, he jerked into a standing position.

There was a knock and the door opened to reveal the Wise Woman with Sol peeking over her shoulder. The Wise Woman shut the door before Sol could enter Rubia's hut behind her. Part of Rubia was very grateful for the reprieve from her curious neighbor. She didn't like the idea of Sol looking at Kyle's naked body. Rubia's gaze slid over to him, but she turned away quickly as heat began to caress her cheeks.

"Rubia, Rubia. You've had a knack for trouble recently, yes?" The Wise Woman knelt at the edge of the bed, holding a small pot filled with an herbal remedy. She placed her hand over the bruised area on Rubia's neck. She chanted a few words before rubbing the herbal ointment over the wound. "You should be feeling well enough soon. It's not too serious."

Rubia nodded. "Thank you, Wise Woman."

"You are most welcome." The Wise Woman's gaze turned to Kyle, and she gave him an assessing once-over. "You have been a fine ally. Don't worry about what is going on right now. Things will become well for you and your people. You will find the happiness you desire."

Kyle inclined his head. "Thank you, Wise Woman."

"Just make sure Rubia gets some rest." She walked a little closer to him and lowered her voice. Words passed between them, and Rubia frowned, wishing she wasn't left out of what they were saying. Could they be talking about her?

She pushed herself into a sitting position and watched as Kyle and the Wise Woman turned their attention to her. "I'd prefer if you didn't whisper in front of me," she said.

"As you wish. I told Kyle the time he has to woo you is becoming increasingly shorter. The Indian males will be arriving tomorrow morning. Of course, this is up to you both, so I don't want to encroach in your business. But it's necessary to make a decision. I do not want to leave you two unaware." The Wise Woman headed toward the door.

"I appreciate you letting us know." Rubia took a deep breath and let it out carefully. "I will take Kyle as a mate," she said and glanced in his direction, "if he will have me."

Kyle nodded, and his eyes widened just a little. "Yes, of course."

The Wise Woman just smiled. "Good. You will find yourself pleased with your decision, Rubia." She turned and walked out, closing the door behind her.

That left Kyle and Rubia alone after the Wise Woman's declaration. Now Rubia wouldn't have the option to turn back. Her raw nerves trembled through her.

Kyle watched her carefully, as if wondering if she would flee from him at any moment. His gaze drifted over her, and she wanted his hands to do the same as they'd done before when they were last alone in her hut.

"You're sure about this?" he asked.

Rubia dipped her head in a nod and pushed into a standing position. She didn't exactly know what to expect. Kyle would lead her toward what they needed to do, though. She gazed into his eyes, and they twinkled with desire.

He crossed the small room toward her and brushed his thumb over her jaw line to her chin. His hand trailed down a little to her neck, away from her wound, and skimmed across her shoulders. He pressed his lips against her bare shoulder and pulled her close. His warm mouth trailed along her skin, up her neck to her lips.

Heat fanned between her legs, and she couldn't stop the moan that trickled from her lips. She placed her hands on Kyle's shoulders and ran them over the hard muscles there. She took a step back, and her calves hit the bed.

Kyle followed.

She broke away from the kiss. Her gaze dipped to take in his male form before she could stop herself. His cock was firm and stretched toward his belly button. She wrapped her hand around the velvety shaft and brushed her thumb over the tip.

Kyle's body tensed visibly, and a groan slipped through his lips. His eyes closed to mere slits, and he tilted his head back. He balled his hands into fists at his sides.

She blinked and watched his reactions as she ran her palm up and down his solid shaft. She squeezed a little harder, and he gritted his teeth.

"Not too much, Rubia. You're... making me very—"

She rubbed her thumb over his tip again, silencing his words. "Very what?"

He stared at her, and a small smile curved his lips. "You'll find out soon enough." He knelt next to her bed and ran his hands over her shoulders to the material covering her breasts. She lifted her arms as he pulled the top from her. He stared at her breasts in wonder and cupped the soft flesh in his hands before pressing his lips against one and then the other.

She brushed her hands through his hair, and his gaze lifted to hers.

His tongue curled over her nipple, and he drew it into his mouth, softly sucking it. Pulling sensations tugged through her body from between her legs as if by a string. His hands went behind her back to help her lay down. He hovered above her on her small bed.

She placed her hands on his neck and tugged him down, wanting to kiss him again.

Kyle's lips met hers, and his mouth ravaged her. He pinned her to the bed, and his hand drifted to her waist. He caressed along her hip and slid his fingers up her thigh under the small skirt covering her.

She gasped as his hand met with her flesh and moved to the point of her body that ached to be filled. Desire flared within her, and she wanted him in ways she'd never imagined before. She wasn't sure how this would change her future, but she was ready to feel what happened between a man and a woman. Especially if that meant being with Kyle. Her protector. Though she didn't feel like she needed protection, he'd been there for her, and his care for her had radiated in his eyes even in his werepuma form.

Rubia spread her legs, and Kyle's hand drifted closer, bringing a gasp to her throat. She stared at him, and he watched her expressions, smiling as she moved beneath his touch. Her lips met his again.

His fingers moved, dipping inside her pussy. She slipped her tongue between his teeth, caressing his tongue with her own. Kyle groaned, deepened the kiss, and pressed his tongue into her mouth, penetrating her lips like he did her lower half. His fingers increased their eager pace.

She leaned back against her pillow, and she squeezed her eyes closed, enjoying the sensation of his touch.

He withdrew, and she peeked her eyes open, sad at the loss. He smiled and spread her legs a little more.

How would she be able to take in the full length of his cock when his finger had filled her so deliciously? She didn't have to wonder for long.

He pressed himself against her and paused. "You're sure about this? Once we do this… there's no going back." Solemnity drew Kyle's brows together, and he watched her as if afraid she'd run away and tell him to stop now.

"I want this, Kyle. And if you think to stop while you've built this delicious fire within me, then I'd have to skin your hide." She smirked at him, and he cocked an eyebrow but shared a grin.

"Well, I wouldn't want that, now, would I?"

She moaned as his cock inched inside her. "No, you wouldn't. I'm quite handy with a knife." She leaned her head back against the pillow, and Kyle brushed kisses along the length of her neck. He soon pressed their bodies together and backed away, then slid in for another long stroke. He began rocking his hips in a slow, torturous pace.

"More, Kyle. Please." She ran her hands through his hair and cradled him close to her, savoring the moment between them.

He sped up his thrusting, and he cupped her breast again, brushing his thumb over the nipple. "You mean so much to me, Rubia. Ever since I first saw you, I've wanted you. How can that be possible?"

"I don't know, but I'm glad you haven't given up on me, especially after the way I've treated you." She ran her hands over his face and cradled it carefully. She smiled and pressed her lips to him. A wave of desire surged through her, and she moaned, feeling the sensation rise to a whole new level as Kyle thrust his hard cock within her. She bit her lower lip.

The soft sound of flesh smacking against flesh and their harsh breathing were the only things to break the silence. Beads of sweat trickled over their bodies as ecstasy crashed over her. She moaned and kissed Kyle to keep from screaming her pleasure and alerting her fellow villagers of what was currently taking place in her home. She didn't want anyone coming in at this time, or the burning awareness that they'd know what she was doing.

Kyle thrust into her a final time and groaned into her mouth as his hot seed burst within her. She ran her hand over his back as he settled on top of her, being conscientious of his weight. She enjoyed the feel of him over her. The sensation she wasn't alone. Her body was weak from the delicious pleasure Kyle had given her, and she couldn't stop the pull of sleep. Letting out a breath, she gave in.

* * *

Kyle brushed a kiss to her forehead as she closed her eyes. He settled the blanket over her again. He sat on the floor next to Rubia's bed and leaned against the wall, not wanting to disturb her.

Sighing, he wished he'd grabbed his clothes from Rubia's hammock before coming back to the village. He needed to go check on what was going on with Jorge and the other werepumas who had betrayed him. Sparing a glance at Rubia, he wondered how he'd divide his time and his life between his new mate and his Pride. Rei was a lucky bastard since he just had to devote himself to Adara and helping her with her tribe instead of thinking about his own people as well as her.

Kyle stood and quietly went to the door. He wouldn't be gone long. He glanced over his shoulder at Rubia. She had a smile on her face, and the glimpse of her curvy body beneath the thin blanket built desire within him again. He pushed it down and turned away. He didn't want the burden of explaining a raging hard-on to the villagers.

He needed to clean off after the workout he and Rubia had just gone through. His gaze scanned Rubia's home, and he found a small bowl of water with a cloth next to it. He cleaned off and then walked out. He strode through the village, doing his best not to feel the slight self-awareness of strutting his stuff through a woman-filled village.

Gazes turned in his direction and talk sounded as he passed through in the torch-lit night. Once he was near the gate, he ran to Rubia's hammock, then grabbed his clothes and put them on. He was a werepuma, and shapeshifters didn't feel the sting of discomfort normal people felt with nudity, but he'd feel more comfortable having his clothes on while he talked with the Amazons and Rei about the justice to be dealt on the rogue werepumas.

Walking back into the village, he spotted Rei near an extra sturdy looking hut with a few Amazon warriors with swords and spears. Kyle inclined his head to Rei and the tribeswomen.

Rei gave a slight grin and cocked an eyebrow.

Kyle couldn't help the easy grin that sprung to his lips. Rei knew what he'd done. He could probably smell the scent of sex on his skin. The Amazon women looked between them in confusion, but they didn't say anything, just stood there stoically.

"So, what is to be done with the hostiles?" Kyle asked.

Footsteps came up behind him, and he turned to see the Adara the Amazon Queen. The Amazon warriors bowed their heads before resuming their positions. Adara gave a soft smile. "We're willing to hear your thoughts. We know you'll distribute proper punishment for their crimes against my tribeswoman and friend. We have disposed of your dead with the help of your Pride." She nodded to Eduardo and the other two

69

werepumas who sat near the bonfire.

"I think the punishment for the injured has already been done. As for Jorge, I think it fair he is put to death if he doesn't feel remorse for his betrayal. I don't think exiling him would be a good option. Not with the importance of secrecy for your people and my own." Kyle didn't want one of his people to be the downfall of them all. He'd rather kill Jorge for his actions, but he wouldn't do so if Jorge was sorry for what he'd done.

He wasn't a harsh dictator, even if that would be the best for his people. They needed someone strong and capable, and he wanted to be that person. Although, he didn't want to risk being hated. Rubia's opinion of him, and the opinion of her people to a lesser extent, meant more to him than exacting perfect justice.

Adara nodded at her warriors, and they went inside the hut to bring out Jorge. An Amazon was on each of his arms with another holding a spear to his jugular. The second looked determined and ruthless. He recognized her as Adara's second in command, Sandi.

He crossed his arms over his chest and watched the traitor vigilantly. If he made even one move to hurt anyone, Kyle would rip his throat out.

Rei moved next to Adara. He obviously didn't like her so near a dangerous shapeshifter, especially while she was pregnant.

"You have betrayed your leader and sought to harm his mate, my friend and tribeswoman. What do you have to say for yourself?" Adara said, her voice commanding and authoritative.

Jorge sneered at her. "You Amazons think you're so powerful." He rolled his eyes. "What do you want me to say?" His gaze shifted to Kyle. "Want me to tell you how sorry I am to a man who desires a piece of ass more than his own people? I should've been the next leader. Not you. I've tried to tell you how to run the Pride. I've taught you what you have to do to be a leader."

Kyle stepped forward. "And as I gave you the chance earlier, you refused to fight me. You refuse because you know I am stronger. That's why I'm the leader of my Pride, and you are not. A worthy leader possesses power, and that's something you're unfamiliar with." He clenched his hands into fists and held them at his sides. He knew Jorge had no remorse for what he'd done, and because of that he would pay with the most severe of punishments.

He looked the man in the eyes and sighed.

"Do what must be done," Adara said from over his shoulder.

He heard footsteps approach. Ones he recognized. Glancing over his shoulder, he saw Rubia standing there and rubbing her eyes. She held her spear in her hand.

"What's going on?" She held beauty he'd never witnessed before. A primal beauty that held power over him and made him desire her. Her eyes widened, and a snarl sounded from Jorge. "Watch out!"

The weight of another body hit his, and he looked to see one of the Amazon warriors thrown to the side. Jorge leapt through the air at him. A whistling sounded near Kyle's head, and the solid thunk of a spear hit Jorge in the chest, halting him. He fell from the air and landed on his side, blood dripping from his lips.

Kyle glanced back to see Rubia staring between him and Jorge. Her eyes were wide, and her mouth was pressed into a thin pink line. Concern wrinkled her forehead.

Adara was at her side and placed her hand against Rubia's shoulder. "It's okay. You did the right thing."

Eduardo and the other werepumas were there within seconds as well. Eduardo stared at the body on the ground, and then Rubia. "Your spear has saved my people from losing yet another leader. Thank you, Amazon."

Rubia looked at him. Her face still filled with shock and concern. She nodded.

Kyle crossed the distance between them and took Rubia into his arms. "Thank you." He pressed a kiss against the top of her head.

"I guess we're even. You saved my life, and I've saved yours." She glanced up at him, and the ghost of a smile brushed her lips.

"Yes. I guess we are." He cradled her close to him and rubbed his hand gently over her back. "I love you, Rubia."

She moved back just enough to look him in the eye. "I love you too."

Adara came to them after another moment. "She needs to rest. I'll take her to my home to do so while you handle the disposal of the dead." She led Rubia away and toward her and Rei's hut.

Rubia watched him as she walked off.

Kyle turned away and looked at Rei, Eduardo, and the other werepumas. Eduardo was already dislodging the spearhead from Jorge's chest with some assistance from Rei.

Once the spear was out of Jorge's chest, Kyle closed the man's eyes. He carried the corpse over to the large fire and set his body into the flames. They stood there and watched him burn.

Kyle needed a new second in command now. He glanced over at Eduardo and suspected he knew who would be a good fit for the job.

6

The next day, Rubia and Kyle set out to the water's edge of one of the tributaries of the Amazon River. Rubia slid out of her outfit and watched as desire lit Kyle's eyes. Her people were careful when they ventured anywhere they could be spotted. They didn't want to be found. There was the chance of great danger.

True, they'd settled down and made their village. They didn't want to be fugitives and on the run from those who would take advantage of them like history had proved.

She started to get in the water, but Kyle grabbed her arm, jerking close to his chest. "There are piranhas in there," he said. His lips were just in front of hers. His breath drifted over her lips, and she leaned in to kiss him.

His hands slid down her body, and he cupped her butt, pulling her into his arms.

She circled her legs around his waist and felt the hard press of him against her through his jeans. She wanted to take him within her again, but that'd have to wait a little. She'd brought him here for the experience of seeing this place, especially after his second in command werepuma had nearly killed him. She didn't like the fact danger could lurk so close to the ones she loved.

Kyle's hand slipped between them to toy with the small button of her clit. He massaged it in tight circles, and she leaned her head against his shoulder, enjoying the feel of him. He made it hard for her to think about moving away from him or about what had happened the night before.

She reluctantly pulled away from him. "The piranha tends to eat dead or injured things. I was born here. I've been taught the precautions to take."

He frowned and ran his hand through his hair. "I know, but I'm not comfortable with that. It's still potentially dangerous."

Rubia sighed. She'd have to show and teach him more about life in the

72

Amazon Rainforest. Once he understood, he wouldn't fear. She stepped over to a blanket he'd laid nearby. She tugged his arm and pulled him down with her.

He raised an eyebrow and laced his fingers behind his head, staring up at her as she straddled his waist. "What are you doing? Not that I mind, of course."

She opened his pants as she'd seen him do previously. "Enjoying you." She leaned down and kissed him, slipping her tongue into his mouth and caressing his tongue with hers. She wasn't quite used to the art of passion, but she knew she'd be a quick learner. Kyle was someone she enjoyed sharing these moments with.

He ran his hands over her body, so he could run his thumb over her clit.

She leaned her head back and moaned, feeling desire and wetness build between her legs. She raised herself up, and Kyle gripped his cock in his fist to guide it into her. She slid down carefully at first. Soon, she needed more of him and took him fully within her.

Kyle groaned. He held her hip with one hand and reached up to massage her breasts with his other hand. Lifting his hips, he met her strokes with his own.

She moved up and down on his cock, a little awkwardly at first, but once she gained her confidence, she rocked her hips, moving against him with fervor.

He closed his eyes, and his lips parted slightly. "God, Rubia. You work your magic on me so well. How do you do this?"

"I can't give away my secrets." She grinned at him, feeling desire flame within her.

He opened his eyes to mere slits and smirked. "Of course not." His face scrunched a little, and his grip on her hips tightened. "Slow down. I'm getting closer."

Her body tightened, and she gasped as passion ripped through her, driving her harder onto him. She bent forward, using her arms to hold herself up. She cried out, and her body spasmed as release took her over.

Kyle grabbed her hips and thrust up into her a few more times as she clenched around his hot cock. He groaned and came inside her.

She rested her forehead against his shoulder. "You make my body feel so good." She settled on top of him and pressed kisses against his chest. "I love being with you like this."

"I love it too. You're the best thing that has happened to me." He trailed his hand over her back in soothing motions.

She glanced at him. "I feel that way about you too. Are you sure I can't influence you to wade a little into the water?"

He pushed up on his elbows and frowned at her. "Well, if either of us gets eaten, I'm holding you responsible."

She laughed and brushed her lips over his. "I wouldn't risk you like that. I... love you." The words felt strange in her mouth, and yet they were so right.

He smiled and pressed his forehead to hers. "I love you too, my mate."

JUNGLE BLAZE

1

S oft moans filtered into her sleep, and Sol Rios blinked open her eyes. Drowsily, she pushed herself into a sitting position and rubbed her hands over her face. Sleep wasn't her friend anymore. Not since her neighbor, Rubia, had mated with the werepumas' leader.

The quiet sighs of pleasure gained intensity and became more insistent, more demanding. Her hands balled into fists.

Dampness and warmth gathered between Sol's legs. She squeezed her thighs together against the cruel sensation.

This was crazy. She had to get away from here. Would it look too suspicious if Sol asked Adara, the Amazon Queen, if she could move her hut? Rubia and Adara were friends. Sol didn't know if there would be a problem, but she would have to come up with a good reason, instead of just complaining about the... noise.

Once dressed, she stepped out into the night.

Darkness blanketed the village, and only a few torches here and there provided light for her to see. She headed toward the center of the village where the Amazons and werepumas held their feasts. Embers glowed hot in the fire pit. She sat beside it, enjoying the heat and the night sounds of the rainforest.

A few guards—both Amazon and werepuma—were prowling the catwalks, and one of the Amazons noticed her with a wave. She returned the kind gesture then lowered her gaze to the coals. Toasty warmth caressed her skin. She wrapped her arms around her legs, hugging them to her chest, and then rested her chin on her knees.

Movement drew her attention away from the fire pit, and she caught sight of a tall, lithe figure striding from the village's entrance toward her. Torchlight revealed his face, and she sucked in a breath. The werepumas' second in command. What was his name again...? Argh, she couldn't remember.

She was thankful for the darkness; otherwise, she'd have run.

Her gaze followed him as he walked past without even looking at her. She buried her face in her legs, wishing she had what the others had. More of her people were finding their mates, yet no one paid her any attention. Especially not the man she found most attractive. He didn't even spare her a glance.

At this rate, her womb would become barren before he even made eye contact. She shook her head, shrugging off any pity for herself. Peeking over her shoulder, she saw the pumas' second in command standing in front of Rubia's hut. Even from this distance, she saw tension in his posture. Maybe Rubia and the werepuma leader were still rutting like wild animals.

Sol turned away before he felt her gaze on him. Not like that would matter much. She hadn't seen him look or talk to any of the other women aside from Adara, Rubia, and a few Amazon guards. All occasions were strictly for business.

He didn't seem to possess much charm or charisma, just a stern, no nonsense attitude, and yet Sol couldn't help the attraction she felt toward him. What was wrong with her?

Faint footsteps approached her from behind, but maybe he was just leaving the village again. It didn't mean he'd have any reason to talk with her. Right? The sudden encompassing silence unsettled her.

Out of the corner of her eye, she saw a pair of denim-clad legs. Her gaze slid up those strong legs and over his solid chest until she stared into his dark blue eyes.

A frown curved his lips, and he folded his arms over his chest. "You live in the hut next to Rubia, don't you?"

Sol froze and looked around as if he could've been talking to an invisible person next to her. His irritated sigh drew her attention back to him. "Ye-yes, I do."

He looked from her to Rubia's hut again. "Give them a message for me when they manage to tear themselves away from each other." Displeasure oozed from his tone.

His gaze pinned her in place, and she felt as small as an ant. At least she'd been wrong about something—her hair wasn't gray nor her womb barren—but this wasn't quite how she'd imagined him looking at her. In her daydreams, he'd been kind and caring, instead of like this.

Any bit of self-confidence she'd once possessed had leaked away. Her nerves shook with the force of his intimidating stare. "Message?" Her voice squeaked. Heat rose to her cheeks, but she fought back the blush.

The sexy werepuma frowned. "Yes, tell them that I—" Shaking his head, he balled one hand into a fist. "Forget it. I'll come back tomorrow."

He walked off. Lowering his voice, he murmured, probably not thinking she'd hear, "The message probably wouldn't reach them if I left it with her. She hardly has any backbone."

Her heart plummeted into her gut, and she clenched her hands into fists. She barely held back her tears. "You don't know me," she said, her words a whisper.

The werepumas' second stopped, and he turned just his head, looking over his shoulder and giving her a great view of his profile. His lips curled back from his teeth a little. "I have no reason to." He strode away, leaving her sitting by the fire pit, alone.

Her emotions shuffled through hurt, humiliation, and finally settled with anger. Pulling herself to her feet, she stared after him. She had her reason for wanting to move her home now, and she'd be petitioning Queen Adara first thing tomorrow.

* * *

Eduardo clenched his fists tight. While he was adamant about distancing himself from these women, he disliked how he'd behaved with the young female. His agitation at finding Kyle, his people's leader, and Rubia, Kyle's mate, in the throes of passion had shot his nerves all to hell.

Ever since mating, Kyle spent more of his time with Rubia than Eduardo thought was necessary. However, Kyle had shown his ability to look after the Pride. He wouldn't be questioning his leader… much. Not after what had happened with the Pride's previous second in command. He grinned.

The feeling of being watched halted him. Turning to where he'd left the woman, he caught her staring at him with fire in her gaze.

Maybe he'd been wrong about her, but that didn't mean anything. Unlike his leader, Eduardo had no interest in binding himself to an Amazon, or any other woman for that matter. He'd loved someone once, but she'd screwed him over when he needed her the most. Never again would he put himself in a position like that.

Although, now he was cursed to be a werepuma. Maybe it was fate. He wasn't meant to be happy.

Stalking past the village's gates and into the forest, he still wasn't sure why Kyle had chosen him from the other werepumas as his second in command. They could barely stand each other prior to the attack on his mate, but his respect for Kyle had increased. He hadn't thought Kyle was a good choice as their leader before, since he'd betrayed their previous leader. He had used his friendship with the weretiger to make an alliance with the Amazon women instead of backing the Pride.

Then Eduardo had realized how poor a decision their former leader had made. Kyle had earned his position, proving, if nothing else, that he had the power to rule. Jorge, the power-hungry former second in command, had filled Kyle in on the basics of leading their people. At least Jorge had accomplished one good thing while he was alive.

Eduardo rolled his eyes and stripped off his clothes. For tonight, he'd shapeshift into his puma form and sleep in a tree. He didn't feel like trekking back to the werepuma camp when he'd need to travel back here in the morning.

He glanced up at the village's catwalks, spotting an Amazonian guard. He slid behind a tree before she could see him. He wouldn't shift in anyone's view. It was his own personal hell to endure. That was how it would stay too.

Anguish radiated through him as he concentrated on reshaping his body. His bones broke, tendons and joints tore, and his skin split open, unleashing a huge, tawny beast.

He huffed when it was over, stretching his feline form, and then leapt into the tree to settle in for the night.

2

Sol cradled her head in her hands. Morning had come, and after last night, she didn't want to face the day and head outside. Not after her first interaction with the werepumas' second in command whom she'd hoped would sweep her off her feet like the other women she envied.

Anger built within her again, replacing self-pity. She was an Amazon. Albeit, her status was unique. She lived between the two social classes of the village. That put her in an awkward position. She was not a warrior or one in any position of influence, but as her mother and grandmother before her, she wasn't at the bottom either. Yet, she mostly had domestic responsibilities such as cooking and crafting clothes.

She knew how to fight—all the women were trained—but she wasn't one of the esteemed who hunted their meals or defended their village.

That wasn't for lack of trying, but no one really gave her much thought. It was almost as if she were invisible most of the time. She shook her head and headed to the door. Before she could open it, someone knocked.

Sol blinked at the door. Who could possibly be visiting her? People rarely came to see her.

The knock sounded again. There was more force behind it this time. If she didn't open the door, the next time they banged on it, her hut might fall in on itself!

She cracked open the door, and right outside stood the werepumas' second in command. Her mouth dropped open, and she stared.

The full force of his gaze slammed into her, and his jaw tightened, showing muscles tic in his cheek. He waited, not saying a word.

She kept watching him, wondering what to do.

He was the last person she'd expected to see darkening her doorstep. So why was he here when he'd made his feelings clear last night?

"Are you going to—" He cocked his head to the side, and a frown darkened his already gloomy expression.

"Eduardo, we need to talk." Kyle's deep, masculine voice came from the direction of Rubia's hut.

She leaned away from the doorframe, staying out of sight.

Spearing her with a sharp look, Eduardo turned away and walked to the other hut.

Sol closed the door quietly, but she pressed her ear against the wooden entrance. Male voices sounded outside, but she couldn't make out their words. Pursing her lips, she imagined he'd now be too busy with Kyle to try to talk with her again.

She built up her confidence, seeking strength from within herself again. Once ready, she walked outside, not looking in their direction. Her focus was straight in front of her as she headed to the throne area where Queen Adara now stood, talking with her guards. Though her baby was due anytime now, the queen still handled most of the day-to-day business in the village herself. It proved her strength to everyone even more.

Sol respectfully kept her distance since she didn't want to intrude on the queen's affairs.

When Adara finally finished talking with her guards, she turned to Sol. "Hello."

"Queen Adara." Sol bowed her head. "I'd like to ask your permission to move my hut. The—" She broke off as Adara's face twisted in pain, and the queen placed her hands over her full stomach. "My queen? Help! Something's wrong with Queen Adara!"

Adara's knees began to give way, but Sol supported her weight so she wouldn't fall.

Within seconds, Rei, Adara's mate, was at her side. His gaze filled with concern, and he carefully lifted the queen into his arms. He sprinted to the Wise Woman's hut, his movements a blur, before Sol could say anything to him.

She ran a hand through her hair. Soon she'd need to start her chores, but for now, she'd take a stroll around the village's perimeter.

After what she'd just witnessed, she needed time to think, especially with the craziness she'd been through regarding Eduardo. Now she wouldn't even be able to change the location of her hut until she could speak with the queen. She'd be forced to continue to hear Rubia and Kyle's mating... and then there was Eduardo. If she wasn't so close to them, maybe he would leave her alone. He'd have no reason to visit her, as he'd so aptly noted. But that didn't explain why he'd shown up at her home today. Could he have come to discuss last night?

She'd wanted him so much. While she could talk herself into thinking it didn't matter if he ever swept her off her feet, it would be a lie. She still wanted him, but how he'd treated her had hurt. Yet she knew the Indian men would arrive in a day or two. Queen Adara had previously postponed them due to the attack on Rubia and the unsettled werepumas, yet she'd heard word around the village that the Indian men weren't happy about the delay.

The Indians and Amazons were tied by tradition and ritual, which her kin was slowly moving away from. Some thought the Indians were now being pushed away.

Overall, Sol didn't think that last part was entirely true. Some women still mated with the Indians, so maybe it was. Besides, why be subjected to mating in the old fashion when you could find someone you cared about and who was with you more than a few times a year?

Sadly, her time was running out. Not having any luck with Eduardo, maybe she could find someone else. She didn't have long, but surely it was possible. Not that Sol hadn't tried before, but sometimes she had a hard time working up her confidence.

Turning a corner, she slammed into a thick muscular chest. Her balance thrown off, she fell backward toward the ground.

Strong arms grabbed her by the waist, holding her up. She gulped and looked into Eduardo's dark blue eyes. Fire scorched between her legs, and she squirmed as his intense gaze bore into hers.

His hands lingered on her, and his gaze trailed down her front. He gritted his teeth, the muscles in his jaw clenching. After removing his hands from her waist, he grabbed her arm, his hand a vise on her as she regained her balance. That took longer than normal due to the raging fire in her belly, which nearly made her swoon at his feet.

Once she was steady, he twisted on his heel then strode away, heading out of the village and deeper into the rainforest.

Sol balled her hands into fists. Irritation clouded her better judgment. How could he just walk away from her like that? What kind of man was he?

She should go back to her mission of finding someone different, but her anger sent her after him, set on finding answers.

3

Eduardo's frustration rose within his chest. Sol's footsteps softly made her presence known, but he wouldn't get into it with her when her kin were around. Although he wasn't sure what was going on between them, he needed to distance himself from her.

He couldn't let her even remotely think that they could be mates. He was not the mating kind. He wouldn't put himself through another serious relationship where he was bound to get hurt. Then again, with how he'd behaved, why would she want anything to do with him?

Finally, he couldn't handle it anymore. He spun on her, pulling her behind a tree when they were just out of earshot of the village and its guards. His hands clenched her upper arms, but he forced himself not to squeeze too hard. Regardless of how he felt, he didn't want to hurt her. He wouldn't use his strength on a female human like that.

Although she looked clearly startled, heat filled her gaze before she looked away from him. Desire wafted from her like a drug. His body tightened, and he jerked away as if burned.

"What is it with you?" he demanded.

"Wh-what?" Confusion wrinkled her brow, but he heard the huskiness in her voice.

"Why do you always watch me with yearning in your eyes?" She looked startled, as if he'd told her something surprising. "I'm not blind." Her mouth opened as if to say something, but he continued, "I'm not someone you'd want a relationship with. You're—"

"How can you or anyone else assume to know what I want? No one pays me any attention. I'm inconsequential—"

Anger burned in Eduardo's gut. She was wrong. How could she think such a thing? Grabbing her by the waist, he pushed her against the tree and kissed the rest of her words away. His tongue thrust between her lips, and she gave a startled squeak. His body pressed against her, and he melted against the sweet curves of her body.

No, he couldn't do this. He jerked away. But a kiss didn't mean he'd take her as a mate. He wouldn't allow himself to be burned like before, but even as he wanted to distance himself, his body craved hers. It had been so long since he'd taken a woman to bed, and now he wasn't sure if he'd be able to restrain himself. Maybe if he got her out of his system, he'd be able to do what he knew he should.

Sol touched her fingers to her slightly swollen lips, but other than that, she stayed still, like she didn't know exactly what to do. Her eyes were wide, and she looked so innocent.

He rubbed his hands over his face, trying to convince himself he didn't need to ravish her like a hungry cat, but his irrational side was winning. The more she stood there looking like that, the less in control he was. The only thing worse would be if she ran. If she did, things wouldn't be pretty.

As if sensing danger, she shuddered and looked away from him, staring in the direction of her village. Her body tensed, and he knew she was prepared to run.

Even as she took her first step, he grabbed her, spinning her face first into the tree. He pressed his hips against her and held himself there. His breathing became ragged, and he tried calming the beast raging within him that demanded he claim her. He clenched his hands into fists and planted them above her head on the tree.

Her hands stretched up and brushed against his. She looked over her shoulder at him. Tendrils of her blonde hair covered her face like a curtain.

His breathing hitched, and he dipped his hands to her small skirt. He shoved it up to her waist, driving a gasp from her throat. His beast rumbled its approval at the sight of her bare backside. He trailed his fingers over her hips to her upper thigh, and she squirmed.

"What are you doing? Eduardo…"

His hand met the patch of fur between her legs, and he dipped a finger between her moist lips. Her protests ceased, and she gasped. Her body reacted to his, and she thrust against his hand.

Encouraged by her reaction, he swirled his finger over her clit, stoking her desire. He pushed her hair to the side, brushing kisses and playful nips along her bare shoulders and neck.

Sol moaned, her body already moistening for him. She leaned her forehead against her hands on the tree. The muscled line of her back drew his gaze to her ass again.

While he wouldn't mind taking his time with her, her scent hardened his cock painfully. There would be nothing pretty and romantic about this.

He unzipped his jeans, needing to be inside her. Gripping her hips, he lifted them for a better angle of entry. His cock slid between the slick folds of her pussy, and he eased himself into her.

His grip on her nearly slipped as he broke through the wall of her virginity. What had he done? Though he didn't know much about the Amazons and their traditions, he should've used common sense, but with her, sense eluded him.

"Ouch! Put me down." She struggled against him, not making him feel any better about his decision to take her like this.

He stilled within her, but his beast was too close to the surface for him to release her. If he wasn't careful, the beast might take control. He took a deep breath and forced himself to relax. "I'm sorry."

"I didn't know this hurt so much. From the way Rubia and..." Her voice trailed off, embarrassment sneaking into it. "Never mind."

He raised an eyebrow, but he rocked his hips against her, taking his time, wanting her to experience pleasure. "No, it shouldn't hurt. I'll be more gentle." He kissed her neck, sweeping his tongue and teeth over her soft skin. "Relax. It'll help."

Sol drew in a deep breath, then let it out slowly. Her tense muscles eased until she didn't feel so rigid.

Gradually, he picked up his pace. Her virginal tightness made him want to slam his cock into her again and again, but he wouldn't hurt her. His feline beast hissed, angry at the lack of hot, hard sex. It wanted to pin her down and claim her, but Eduardo wasn't up to the task with a virgin. That wasn't the impression he wanted to make.

She pressed against him as he thrust harder and faster into her. His hands clenched her hips, keeping her steady while she held on tight to the tree in front of them. Moans poured from her throat. He drove himself into her, his hips smacking against hers. With each thrust, he drew closer to the edge, but he refused to claim her as a mate. He wouldn't do that to himself or her.

She leaned her head back, placing it against his chest. Sweat trickled along their skin, slickening their bodies, from both passion and the jungle's heat. He adjusted his weight and wrapped his arm around her waist, holding her with one arm so he could use his free hand to toy with her clit again.

He wiggled his finger against the sensitive nub, and her pussy tightened around his cock. She gasped, her cries of passion gained volume, and while their argument would've been fine at this distance, he wasn't certain this would be.

Eduardo withdrew his hand from between her legs, and he covered her mouth at the start of another loud moan. He slammed his cock deeper, taking her completely.

She froze, her body spasming, and he tightened his grip on her while she rode out the orgasm. He was close. So... close.

Pulling out of her, he released his load on the ground between their legs.

Not filling her with his seed displeased him, but it was better this way. He rested his forehead against her shoulder and released his grip on her mouth. She relaxed a little, but her posture was once again stiff, a little uncertain.

He arranged her mini-skirt back around her hips again, trying to make her feel more comfortable. Although he wasn't exactly sure how to do that with what had just occurred between them. The one thing he knew was how much he'd enjoyed himself. Once might not be enough, but was she worth letting himself be vulnerable again?

He wanted to say no, but something about her refused to let things be that simple. If they'd been in the city and lived like most people, he wouldn't think twice about having his way with her occasionally. The Amazons' culture was different. They mated with one person until death. That was one of the few things he'd learned of her kind.

Sol turned around and looked up at him. Her gaze was a little unfocused, and her skin had a pretty pink blush to it. "Are we mates now?" she asked, uncertainty thick in her voice.

* * *

Sol noticed the quick change in Eduardo's demeanor from relaxed and satisfied to the hardened way he looked now. The way he'd looked before all of this. Dark and unhappy.

His lips were drawn tight into a sneer, and he pinched the bridge of his nose. "No. This was a one-time event." He turned away, and she grabbed his arm to keep him from leaving her.

How could he deny her from ever having this kind of pleasure again?

He whirled on her, pinning her to the tree without any of the care he'd displayed before. His gaze bore into hers. "Leave this alone. I'm not interested in you like that. I've had things happen to me before. I won't put myself in the hands of some Amazon woman who doesn't know much about anything."

Her eyes widened at his words. They felt a little too close to the truth. Something she faced on a normal basis. She didn't like feeling insubstantial, and he'd told her she was. Now she just wanted to go hide somewhere.

She struggled against him, and he relinquished his grip on her. Right about now, she didn't care if she ever found a mate or not. If this was how having a man in her life would be, then she didn't want one. She ran, not heading back to her village and not going anywhere near Eduardo.

"You shouldn't go off on your own," he called from behind her.

She ignored him, dismissing his words.

"Your call. If something happens, it's your fault." Eduardo's voice chilled her regardless of the heat.

Sol ventured deeper into the forest. Once she was far enough away, she slumped against a tree and put her face in her hands.

How had she been this stupid? He'd seemed so sincere when he was pleasuring her, and yet he'd just used her, giving her something sweet only for there to be no possibility of having more. Her body still tingled with the delicious sensations, and that made her even sadder.

Grimacing, she pushed into a standing position. She didn't want to deal with anyone. If she ran away from her village, no one would notice she was gone.

She scowled. There might be some who missed her. Like those she made clothes and other things for. She gazed up at the tall tree behind her then climbed up onto one of the sturdier branches. Soon enough she'd figure out what she would do. Right now, she just needed time to relax.

Settling in, she leaned her head against the tree. The chance of finding a mate and having a happy life like the other mated females in her village lessened by the moment. She'd become one of those who kept the Indian men happy, and that was all.

Her happiness wouldn't matter.

4

The next morning dawned, and worry gnawed at Eduardo's chest.

He crossed his arms as he scanned the crowd. Yesterday afternoon had been the last time he'd seen Sol since she left him. He was beginning to regret the way he'd treated her. If he hadn't been such a jerk, she wouldn't have run away.

The Amazon queen's new baby girl had the tribe stirred up with happiness, and no one, aside from him, had acknowledged Sol's absence. He felt for Sol, and from what he saw, maybe she hadn't lied about being invisible to those around her.

He couldn't leave the village since he had orders from Kyle to help make sure everything went smoothly. With Adara in her weakened state, they needed to be their strongest. The Indian men were due to arrive a little later today. The Amazons couldn't turn them away again. Too much conflict lay that way, so instead, the werepumas were to help act as guards for the queen.

As time passed, he finally reached his limit. If he couldn't find her himself, he would have one of his men do it for him. He strode to Jaime, one of the younger pumas, but Kyle reached them before Eduardo could talk to the younger man.

"Is everything okay?" Kyle asked, looking between them. From his keen gaze, he knew something was going on, but he didn't know what.

"It's fine," Eduardo said. He waited, hoping not to have to answer any more questions. Fortunately, Kyle nodded and walked back to Rubia, who was near the bonfire. He turned his gaze back to them but shrugged it off.

"So what's wrong?" Jaime struggled to keep concern off his face, obviously trying to keep Kyle from noticing them again. Jaime wasn't one to go against Kyle, but he and Eduardo had a good understanding. He trusted the guy.

He opened his mouth to tell Jaime to go find Sol, but his gaze caught movement toward the gates. A tired-looking Sol trudged through the crowd and headed for her home, barely interacting with anyone around her.

Eduardo stepped away from Jaime. "Nothing. Never mind," he said, his voice sounding distant.

He made his way toward her, but the Wise Woman reached her before he had a chance to at least apologize for his harshness the previous day. For reasons unknown to him, worry had consumed him last night, and he'd had a hard time sleeping.

He could've gone to her, but he would've had to track her, and with the way they parted, he hadn't wanted to argue with her and drive her farther away from him. Ever since their first conversation the other night, things between them had been tense and awkward. But he wasn't ready for a relationship.

Even as he thought that, he watched Sol and the Wise Woman. Sol's tiredness evaporated into something akin to dread or concern. What was going on? What brought on that look?

Her gaze skimmed the crowd and then connected with his. Her shoulders tightened; she nodded her head to the Wise Woman and said one last thing to her before retreating to her hut, slipping inside before anyone else could corner her.

Damn. He'd missed his chance. He couldn't talk with her now when he had to be on the lookout for trouble.

Jaime stepped to his side. "Lady trouble?" he asked. "I didn't know you were forming a relationship with anyone."

Eduardo grimaced. "I don't know." He wasn't convinced he was forming a relationship with her, but he knew there was something between them. He'd just have to wait until later to talk with her. "Get back to your position. We need to be alert."

He turned, but he couldn't help the draw toward her hut tugging at his chest. He'd thought he would never do this to himself again, so what had gone wrong? Shaking his head, he watched the crowd.

A shout from the catwalks returned his attention to the gate. Darkly tanned men appeared there as if from the trees, and he felt very unsettled. But he had to remind himself they were only there to fulfill their end of a bargain the Amazons and Indians had had going on for centuries. It had helped both races' populations until the Amazon queen had found her own mate and then struck an alliance with his werepumas. Now their bargain teetered on a slippery edge.

Eduardo wasn't quite sure how that was going to go.

Sandi, Adara's second in command, greeted them along with the Wise Woman. They walked a little away from the current festivities, which were around the bonfire. Queen Adara and her baby girl weren't out for them.

They were currently staying in Adara's hut, but he figured they'd probably be going to Rei's cabin, which was a little more modern and comfortable, once things settled down.

Eduardo watched the Amazon women and the Indian men walk and talk. The men carried spears, and they strode to different huts, which he presumed housed the unmated women who would soon come into womanhood. He'd heard the women would no longer be available to mate since, once they were claimed, they were off-limits.

He watched as an Indian placed his spear against the front of a hut and walked inside, then another did the same, and another as they made their way around the village. They closed in on Sol's hut, and his palms began to sweat.

"Eduardo," Kyle called.

He glanced back at the werepuma leader to see him waving Eduardo over. He had a smile on his face, which was probably connected to Rubia's mischievous look. They were happy together, and while they'd had several critics, himself included, it was good to see their leader content—and stable. He headed toward them, curious why he was called over.

"Why so serious, Eduardo?" Rubia asked. "This is a celebration." She smiled and wrapped her arms around Kyle's waist.

Eduardo shrugged. He didn't want to talk about his tumultuous feelings for Sol. He could just anticipate what they might say. Instead, he tried to keep his face neutral, but he felt it cracking. He glanced over his shoulder. A spear lay against the side of Sol's hut. He fell to the ground. Agony lashed through his body. His bones snapped, muscles ripped, and his skin split open, pouring fur over his new body.

He tore up the distance between where he stood and Sol's hut, but his eyes spotted tan fur as it veered in front of him, and a hiss of anger slid from Kyle's feline lips. Eduardo tossed his head to the side, urging his leader away, but Kyle didn't budge. Fury flooded his veins.

He circled to one side, trying to throw Kyle off, but Kyle didn't fall for it. He held his ground in front of the hut.

A soft sound came from inside, and Eduardo's beast took over. He leapt over Kyle even as claws slid into his vulnerable abdomen. Eduardo smashed into the door, annihilating it in a blast of materials. The hut swayed over them wearily.

Sol's skirt was pushed up her hips, exposing her to the Indian male who stared at him with wide eyes. Sol screamed and scrambled into a sitting position, and a second after, Eduardo was slammed into the thin wall, which wasn't strong enough to take the brunt of two werepumas. The hut collapsed in on them in a storm of debris.

Weight pushed on his back, and he shook debris off to get himself standing. He needed to get to Sol and make sure she was okay. His sensitive ears heard a muffled feminine whimper, and he limped toward it, not feeling too well.

Kyle's heavy paw landed between his shoulders and pushed him down. Eduardo collapsed to his stomach. He struggled up to no avail then put all his concentration into shifting back into human form. Fingers would be more help than paws to dig Sol out from the hut.

Kyle's claws clenched against his skin, but he felt his leader begin his own shift back.

Eduardo crawled to where he'd heard the whimper and pulled planks of wood away to uncover Sol. When her face and shoulders were out, he pulled with his remaining strength, clearing her from the debris.

Her eyes wide, she stared up at the canopy of trees. She had scratches here and there, but it appeared she was just in shock.

Noise to his side drew his attention, and he saw Kyle helping the Indian man. Kyle's gaze was all for Eduardo. He looked confused and severely unhappy.

Eduardo couldn't blame his leader. He didn't quite know what had come over him, but the thought of Sol being taken away from him forever had his beast reacting before he had a chance to.

Maybe his beast knew something he didn't.

The Indian male didn't look happy either. He looked startled and furious. Not what Eduardo needed right now.

He lifted Sol into his arms, and even that action took more out of him than he'd ever imagined. He felt so weak from shapeshifting twice in a row and from the fight. Blood slicked his naked stomach, and he started to walk away.

Angry chatter in a language he didn't know came from over his shoulder.

The Indian man pointed his finger at Eduardo and shook his head over and over.

"Eduardo, put the girl down," Kyle said. "I don't know what's gotten into you, but you don't have a right to her." He frowned, and his gaze drifted over to Rubia. "You had your chance."

Sol rubbed her eyes and looked up at Eduardo. Surprise lit her eyes. Under that was a flicker of hope, but she turned her head away before he could see much more.

"I do have a right to her." Eduardo looked at the staring crowd. "I've already had sex with her."

Sol flinched, the muscles of her back and shoulder tensing into knots.

"Is this true, Sol?" the Wise Woman asked. Her gaze held curiosity and a little disapproval. The old woman kind of creeped him out since she always seemed to know more than she let on to.

Sol jerked her head in a nod as if she wasn't exactly happy to admit it.

"Then she has been claimed if he has given her his seed." The Wise Woman stared at them for a moment longer and waited, as if expecting them to say something. When neither of them did, she spoke to the Indian man in the other language.

Sol froze in his arms. She opened her mouth but stopped. Her hands pushed against his chest in a struggle to be released.

He hadn't come inside of her. In that way, they weren't exactly mated. He cursed himself inwardly. Did the Wise Woman somehow know that? What was he supposed to do now? Should he claim her like he should've before, or should he admit the truth? He didn't want to admit the truth because she'd be out of his reach forever, and yet, he'd been hurt so badly before. But he couldn't let that excuse stand in the way of a possible life with Sol. One way or another, she'd managed to break through his defenses and make him want her.

The only problem was… what if she no longer wanted him? Would he be able to handle that?

5

Sol stood on her own two feet and pushed down her skirt. What was she supposed to do or say? She pinched the bridge of her nose, staring between the wreckage of her only home and the naked man who'd caused it to be no longer standing.

Yet he'd come for her, and part of her was exuberant for that. Why had he done it? What had changed? Why now? She'd just begun to accept the inevitable, and then here he was giving her hope for something he seemed adamantly against.

She could've told the Wise Woman he'd never given her his seed, but she didn't think that would be such a good idea. Although the Wise Woman seemed to know something, in her mystic ways. But Sol didn't have enough energy to think much into her potential problem.

Besides, who would want her now that she'd already had sex with him? And the whole darn village knew, because they were staring!

She just wanted to curl up on her bed and throw the blankets over her head, but she couldn't because her bed was buried under her hut. She ran a shaky hand through her hair, shoving the loose strands out of her face.

Eduardo watched her intently. Her nerves were near collapse. She wasn't sure she could handle his gaze on top of everyone else's.

A hand descended on her shoulder, and she spun to face Rubia, who wore a concerned frown. "Are you okay?" she asked.

Sol opened her mouth to say something, but words refused to come out. Instead, she shook her head.

Rubia pulled Sol against her shoulder, offering her support, and walked away from the crowd to her hut.

Sol still felt Eduardo's eyes on her back, but she was relieved to have an escape from everyone. They entered Rubia's hut, and she felt immediate relief.

Rubia directed her toward the low table and chairs, and she sat, grateful to be out of sight. "Why didn't you tell the Wise Woman that you had already been claimed, Sol?" The other Amazon sat in front of her, looking concerned.

"I... I don't know. I've just been so confused." She placed her elbows on the table and rested her head in her hands. "It's hard to know what to do, especially..." She pressed her palms into her forehead, frustration weighing her down.

"Especially what?" Rubia placed her hand against Sol's arm. She was being nicer to her than probably ever before. Not that Rubia was rude, but like everyone else, she just didn't see her or something.

"I don't even think Eduardo likes me. After we..." She let out a long breath. "After our time together, I thought we would be together, but he pushed me away. He told me he didn't want to have a relationship. I guess I took him at his word that he didn't want me. The fact he burst into my hut was surprising. How was I supposed to know he'd do that?" She looked up at Rubia.

The other woman frowned. She looked confused as well, like she wished she knew what to say but didn't.

A couple of brisk knocks on the door, and then it opened to reveal Kyle. Behind him stood Eduardo. The look on Kyle's face was like nothing Sol had seen before. He looked pretty pissed off.

Once they were in and had the door closed, Kyle swung on Eduardo. "What the hell do you think you're doing?" he said, his voice low enough that they wouldn't be overheard from the outside. He blocked Eduardo from joining them at the table.

Eduardo stood tall and puffed out his chest. His gaze drifted to Sol before focusing back on Kyle. The two men were both still nude, and Sol averted her eyes, keeping them on either Rubia or the back of the hut. She felt too aware to watch them argue, even though she'd now seen three men naked. But it just wasn't within her comfort zone, and apparently Rubia felt the same way.

"I can't believe you're being this hard on me after your adventure when it came to finding your mate." The sound of a fist smacking flesh rang out before a thud.

Out of the corner of her eye, Sol saw Rubia jump to her feet. She turned to see Eduardo on his butt. His cheek was split, and a trickle of blood ran down it toward his chin. He stared up at Kyle defiantly.

Kyle's back muscles were tense, and Sol knew he was about to strike again. She dove for the two men. Kyle had already started coming, and she was knocked out of the way.

Rubia grabbed Kyle by the arm, and he stopped. His breath came out in pants. "Don't talk about that. I know your opinion. I thought your attitude was firmly in the past," Kyle said, his tone harsh.

Slight pain from being shoved aside lingered in Sol's back, but she was fine. Eduardo's hand descended on her arm, and he gently pulled her to him.

"It is. I'm not the best when it comes to my feelings, but somehow I feel something for her. When we were first together, I thought it'd be a one-time deal, but obviously there's something about her that won't let go of me." He glanced at her, and emotions shone in his blue eyes.

She didn't know how to take this. It was something she'd wanted too badly, and now it was happening. She almost wondered when something would go wrong. That seemed to be how her life went. Well, there was something wrong. Her lack of a home now. All caused by Eduardo.

What did he want from her? At first, he thought she was nothing, then there was something between them, but he pushed her away, and now he wanted her? She was so confused.

Her gaze dropped to his bleeding stomach, and she noticed his golden skin had paled a few shades. She blinked, staring at his wounds, then it hit her suddenly. He needed his wounds tended to. His kind healed faster than humans, but that didn't mean they were invincible.

She thought to go for her home where she knew she had meager supplies, but they would do her little good broken and buried. Her gaze rose to Rubia's, and the other woman nodded, taking off outside for the Wise Woman.

Kyle sighed and dropped to the floor next to them. He rubbed the back of his neck and sighed. "You're right. I didn't know what you were doing. For all I knew, you'd lost it and were going to attack the two of them. Especially considering your previous opinion about becoming involved with someone."

Eduardo sighed. "Sorry for the scare."

Shaking his head, Kyle laughed. "It's fine. Just don't do it again, or next time I might not be as gentle." Even as he said it, Kyle's gaze dropped to the rather deep-looking wounds on Eduardo's abdomen. Sol almost thought she saw a little worry in his eyes.

Eduardo shifted on the ground, but Kyle pushed him down by his shoulder. "You're not going anywhere right now. You need bandaging first."

Eduardo stared at him with a frown as if Kyle were being silly, but he stayed there. His gaze turned to Sol, and her insides started to melt a little like they used to when she saw him around the village. She might've finally found someone special who paid attention to what she needed and to her feelings. She wasn't sure. However, the way he'd broken into her place had been pretty impressive.

He pulled her down to him gently and placed a kiss against her lips. It was slow and sweet, something she could get used to. Her body warmed into sweet desire like when he'd held her against the tree and thrust inside her.

She placed her hand against his cheek, caressing the short stubble lining his jaw. The roughness reminded her of the man, and she lost herself in the kiss as it gained intensity.

Kyle coughed.

Eduardo pulled away a moment before the door swung open, and she looked up to see Rubia and the Wise Woman. Their gazes were on Eduardo and the red stain soaking his skin. Looking at the wound, Sol noticed it didn't look quite as life-threatening as it had, but it still needed to be treated. She started to move out of the way, but Eduardo grabbed her wrist, holding her in place. She stayed there with him.

The Wise Woman looked between them as she set her things down. She pursed her lips a little as if seeing something intriguing. The Wise Woman was known to know things others had no clue about, and she didn't let anyone else know about them either. Except maybe her granddaughter who would one day carry on her position. The mother had died during childbirth, which was not uncommon here.

It was something Sol worried about a little as well, but continuing their people was their focus, and it was important.

The Wise Woman went to work on Eduardo's wounds, taking care of them with almost effortless efficiency as she chanted over him. When she was done, she speared Sol with a look.

"I'm sorry, Wise Woman. I should've said something before." The words spilled out of her mouth before she could control them.

"What you did could've led to something terrible. Our mating rituals are sacred among our people. If the Indian had lain with you after you'd already mated with Eduardo, you would've been inviting disaster upon yourself. Do you understand?"

Sol bit her lip. She hadn't quite realized that, but at the time, with Eduardo chasing her away, she hadn't thought it would be much of a big deal. Besides, he hadn't exactly shared his seed with her, right? She wouldn't exactly have invited disaster, or…?

She had no idea. She felt out of her depth. What she knew well was creating clothing and doing domestic chores. All of these emotions and mating things weren't everyday happenings.

"I understand, Wise Woman." She bowed her head, and a gentle, wrinkled hand cupped her chin, tilting her head back up.

The Wise Woman smiled at her. "There's no harm right now. You've found a mate, and he'll make sure to keep you." Her gaze lowered to Eduardo; something slid through her eyes that made him tense, then her focus slid back to Sol. "Your only concern right now, I'd imagine, would be on your ruined home. I'm sure some of the other Amazons will help you rebuild."

Sol figured they would as well. The village was always helpful when Amazons were in need. She wondered what exactly she should be doing now since she felt a little awkward all of a sudden. Kyle, Rubia, the Wise Woman, and Eduardo all looked at her, and she nodded to them before standing.

Eduardo's hand circled her wrist and stopped her. "Where are you going?" His face showed concern.

"I need some air." She smiled, trying to pretend nothing was wrong, but she shouldn't have been surprised when he attempted to sit up and pull her closer.

The Wise Woman placed a hand on his shoulder, keeping him down. "Regardless of your healing powers, you're not well enough to be moving too much. If there's more need of my presence, you all know where I'll be." She packed up her things and left.

Sol felt a little relief, but Kyle and Rubia were still there. While she normally felt awkward around them, the recent admission of her sexual interaction with Eduardo made her feel that much more exposed and uncomfortable. She went around feeling so uptight about how people might view her; it was so crazy.

"Stay with me," Eduardo said from the floor.

"No, I..." Sol looked at Rubia and Kyle, who discreetly watched them while they sat at Rubia's table. She glanced back at Eduardo knowing she didn't want her stuff ruined during the next rain. "I need to start getting my things together." She pulled away from him and moved out of arm's reach before he could try grabbing for her again, then she backpedaled out the door.

Her ruined hut lay crumpled on the ground, looking sad and neglected. Sol crouched beside the pile of sticks, feeling overwhelmed at the heartbreaking task. Taking a deep breath, she moved things around, tossing wood and building supplies to one stack and putting her belongings in another. She went about working, zeroing in solely on what she needed to do and trying to get her mind off everything else. When she looked up, there were other Amazons helping, mostly by pulling the building materials away, letting her handle her own possessions.

She picked up a few of her belongings and put them in a stack with everything else she could salvage. A lot of the more fragile items she'd kept out were ruined, but some of what she'd stored away in her chest survived.

Her gaze remained low since she still caught sight of others looking at her and whispering amongst themselves. A presence came up beside her, and at first, she didn't bother to see who it was, but it remained there nearby.

She looked up then to see the Indian male she'd been given to standing next to her. He wore a frown and kept watching her.

"It's a shame," he finally said. She understood their native language, but she wasn't as good as some of the others.

"I'm sorry?" What was he talking about? Had she misheard something?

"Such a good girl mating with an animal." His face twisted in disgust, and he spat at her feet, barely missing them. "You were destined to lie with me. Not that beast." He reached out for her, but she dodged his grip. One of the werepumas—the one she'd seen Eduardo talk to earlier—stepped between them. Wasn't his name Jaime?

"Leave her alone. She's not yours now." This werepuma seemed more around her age, whereas Eduardo was a few years older.

The Indian male stood up straighter and narrowed his eyes at Jaime as if he wasn't a man qualified to handle this disagreement. As if he were forced to deal with a boy.

Sol started around him, but the werepuma held up a hand to block her.

"No, let me handle this. I'll protect you." Jaime took a step toward the Indian when out of nowhere a breeze tickled her cheek, then there was a solid thump and hot, sticky fluid splashed against her face and upper torso.

From Jaime's back, she saw a jagged point sticking out. His legs gave way, and he collapsed toward her. She reached out to catch him, but a whistling sound similar to what she'd just heard before the werepuma went down had her throwing herself to the ground. Behind where she'd stood, another Amazon had a spear sticking out of her abdomen.

Shouts rang out through the village, and hands jerked her to her feet. Her feet dragged the ground as someone pulled her away from the calamity. Her gaze rose to see darkly tanned skin. She kicked her captor in the back of the leg as he ran for the village gate.

A low, fierce rumble sounded ahead, and she saw two big, tawny cats blocking their way, crouched and ready to pounce. Her captor swung her around, pressing her back tightly to his front. He pressed a sharp blade to her throat, pushing it against her painfully.

A trickle of blood slid down her already bloody neck and torso. The Indian's grip on her tightened, and she gave an involuntary squeak.

The pumas became that much more agitated at the sound. Movement caught the corner of her eye, and Sol saw Kyle striding toward her and her captor. He looked pissed off. His eyes darkened with anger, and she noticed when the Indian spotted him because the Indian jerked, cutting into her neck a little.

She bit her lower lip, holding back a whimper of pain.

The pumas moved a step forward, catching the Indian's gaze, but Sol kept hers on Kyle. She knew he was the bigger threat. She'd seen the aftermath when he'd fought against his own pumas before. While the

Indian men had their own advantages, they were weak compared to him and his kind.

"Let us pass, and I won't kill her," the Indian said.

Kyle's lips tightened, but he didn't say anything. He just watched them. The pumas didn't move an inch. Although she noticed they each glanced at Kyle for orders. When he finally raised his hand, they moved aside.

Anger darkened his eyes, but he had to have a plan. Right? He wasn't letting the Indian have her to teach Eduardo some kind of lesson, was he?

Hope faded in her chest, and she wished she'd thought to do something earlier. She was the one who should've been taking care of herself. The Indian's grip loosened a little, but not by much, and he started forward, followed by other Indians.

Around her, she saw other Amazons and werepumas, but no one did anything. Rubia's gaze caught hers, and anger clenched her neighbor's jaw.

Sol ground her teeth, hoping someone, anyone, would help her. Why weren't they helping her? She didn't know what the Indians would do to her if she was taken away, and from the fact one of them had thrown a spear at her, she didn't think he'd stick with what he'd said about not killing her. Why would they have thrown a spear at her if they hadn't wanted to hurt her?

They edged closer to the gate, and she knew it was critical for her to do something. She slammed her head back against the Indian's face. Her hands grabbed his wrist, and she jerked it away from her, twisting his arm and causing it to make a loud pop. She grabbed the knife from him and dropped into a fighting stance.

The Indian looked at her in surprise like he couldn't believe she'd done such a thing. Out of her peripheral vision, she noticed the Indian men crowding in toward her. They weren't happy about her attack on one of their own.

A low feline rumble sounded beyond the Indians, and her gaze followed the noise to see Eduardo holding a hand against his stomach as he made his way toward them.

A knife blade slammed into her lower back, unleashing a torrent of agony. Her strength faded, her knees buckling.

Shouts erupted, and she saw the blurred violence around her as her body toppled forward. She hit the ground hard. Wetness pooled in the small of her back, and she caught sight of huge felines ripping into fighting Indian males.

Her eyelids became too heavy to keep watching, and they slid closed. A small, calloused hand slid over her back, and she wondered who it was, but she couldn't be bothered with finding out.

The thought of drifting off into the cozy darkness of sleep weighed too heavily on her.

6

Eduardo's gaze focused on Sol on the ground with a dagger sticking out of her back and Rubia next to her. He roared and grabbed the Indian closest to him by the throat, squeezing until he crushed the man's neck. The man crumpled to the ground like a discarded doll.

Kyle leapt at the Indian male who had stabbed Sol in the back, and Eduardo ran forward, wanting his own part in the man's destruction, except he noticed that Sol didn't seem to be moving much now. His heart skipped a beat, and he stumbled back to Sol, falling to his knees beside her.

Rubia looked up at him with a grim look on her face. "We need to get her to the Wise Woman. It's too dangerous for the Wise Woman to come to her with all the fighting."

He nodded and picked up Sol, cradling her in his arms even though his stomach burned from the healing wounds. The fighting continued around them, and Eduardo dodged a werepuma as it struck an Indian about to attack him and Sol. A spear thumped into another Indian male who stood in front of him.

He glanced to the side to see Rubia there, panting with adrenaline. She ripped the spear from the man's chest and led the way. In the distance, he saw the Wise Woman standing near a hut wringing her hands in front of her. Her face was twisted with regret and sadness.

Rei's loud roar seized every muscle in his body from the ferocity of it, and he chanced a glance to see Rei, Queen Adara's mate, in weretiger form. The weretiger ran toward the battle, tearing up the distance between him and the men with his arms and legs eating up the ground. Behind him, Eduardo saw Sandi, Adara's second in command, charging toward the battle with a spear and a knife in her hands.

The Indians and even some werepumas in the vicinity panicked, taking off at a run. Kyle grabbed an Indian man as he ran past and pinned him to the ground. The man shouted at the others in his native language and flailed his arms. Fear glistened in his wide eyes.

A shiver from Sol, and a tug on his elbow from Rubia, sent Eduardo moving again. He needed to get Sol to the Wise Woman, and then he'd need to be back here with Kyle, even though it pained him to be away from Sol. But his place was as Kyle's second in command.

The Wise Woman walked toward them as they moved away from the danger. She looked concerned.

He glanced down at Sol again to see how pale her skin was. He cursed himself for getting so caught up in his surroundings. Without any more thought, he rushed into the Wise Woman's hut at her guidance and set Sol onto the bed laid out for her. He started to stand, but Sol gripped his hand weakly, looking up at him with fear in her eyes.

He knelt again next to her, but he remained out of the way so the Wise Woman could begin her work. "You're going to be okay," he said.

"I don't feel so good. Stay with me." She groaned and held onto him.

The Wise Woman placed her hand on Sol's, pulling the young woman's hand away from Eduardo's and clucking her tongue. "You know he can't stay, little one."

Pain struck him in the chest at the loss of contact with Sol.

The Wise Woman nodded her head. "He is needed by his leader. Besides, you're in no position to have him here. I must focus while I treat you." She waved her hand, and he stumbled to his feet, not feeling like the graceful predator he was at all.

Rubia knelt where he'd been. Her gaze was concerned, and she lowered her eyes.

"Child, I need my herbs. You will help me." The Wise Woman began chanting and turned her full attention to Sol, who watched Eduardo with sad eyes.

He had to get out of here, yet he really didn't want to. With a frown, he pushed open the door and left.

The Indians were mostly dead or gone. Although he noticed several of the werepumas were also absent. They'd probably gone off to kill any who had fled. At least, that's what he'd have ordered, and knowing how Kyle was... well... Go figure.

In the field in front of him, members of his pride were helping the Amazonian women with the dead and wounded, while others prowled the catwalks keeping an eye on their surroundings to make sure they didn't suffer yet another attack.

Someone would pay for this breach. Anger burned within his gut, drawing his beast to the surface. He squeezed his hands into fists then tried to relax again.

Pushing his beast aside, he walked to where Kyle, Rei, and Sandi stood near the gates. The momentum of the battle still tingled within his chest.

Stepping next to Kyle, Eduardo crossed his arms and stared down at the Indian.

"Sandi, whatever agreement your races had has changed. If any of their men make it back to their village, they'll know what transpired here. The agreements you had are gone, leaving the Amazons vulnerable," Kyle said. "I have full confidence in my men catching them, but someone could slip through."

"Yes, but our traditions teach us to avoid confrontation. That is how we've survived this long." Sandi frowned at the Indian who was still pinned down by Kyle.

"They attacked and hurt your Amazons and my werepumas with little hesitation. They'd rather have her dead than let her go. Real men do not attack the mate of another." Kyle's jaw clenched. That hit close to home for him. "And an attack of a mate of my Pride is an attack on the Pride itself."

"We all need to calm down and think about this," Rei said, finally speaking up.

Eduardo felt anger emanating from Kyle. His posture remained tense, but he kept himself in check.

"I agree with Kyle," Eduardo said. "With Adara resting and the Indians retreating, we need to ensure the village will be safe. The Indians could build their numbers and come back to wipe us all out." At Kyle's and Rei's looks, he held up his hands. "Not that we'd make it easy for them, but they could tell the outside world about us. They know where we are."

"You make a wise point." Sandi sighed and looked around the village. "I dare not disturb the Wise Woman with this while she is tending to the wounded."

"With what?" Adara asked, cradling her tiny infant swaddled in a thin cloth. Her gaze took in the blood and bodies. Anger tightened her eyes and lips.

Rei spun around and wrapped his arm around Adara carefully. "You two shouldn't be up and about too much." He frowned at her, but his face warmed when he saw his baby girl.

"The village could be in jeopardy, Queen Adara," Sandi said. "Things didn't go well with the Indian men. They killed one of our women and nearly abducted and killed another. Some of the werepumas and our kin are now injured. We suspect if they reach their village—"

Adara held up her free hand, cutting off Sandi's words. Her attention rested on the Indian at their feet. She spoke to him in their language, and Sandi's frown increased.

Eduardo didn't know what the hell was going on now, but he hoped the Amazon queen knew what she was doing.

After a few moments, she looked at Kyle. "Release him."

"What?" Kyle shook his head. "No, I need to know what's going on."

Adara leveled him a stern look that was pretty damn intimidating for someone gently cradling an infant in her arms. "I'll fill you in."

7

Sol blinked her eyes open to see the inside of the Wise Woman's home. Sadness gripped her chest, and she winced against the pain in her torso.

The Wise Woman leaned into view with her wrinkled skin and kind eyes. "Hello, little one. I'll give you something for the pain, but I need you to listen to my only request. Yes?"

She nodded her head, willing to do anything to end some of her pain. "Yes, Wise Woman."

"Your mating to the werepuma is not complete. You and I both know what must be done for it to be official." The Wise Woman patted her hand, but her expression had hardened, with pinched eyes and downturned lips. "There was conflict between our people and the Indians over your actions. While our queen has mended some of that with a declaration of a truce, it will not be permanent—that I have foreseen."

The full weight of what had happened because of her not saying that Eduardo hadn't shared his seed hit her. If only she'd—

"No, child. I know that look. Do not let the burden weigh on you too heavily."

Sol grimaced, shame and guilt lodged in her throat. "But if you foresaw that my mating with Eduardo wasn't complete, then why didn't you say anything and stop what happened?"

"There is a bright future waiting for you and Eduardo, if only you both would take charge and make that happen. Sometimes change is necessary, even for our kind." She smiled, and the stern look melted away. "Now then, I know someone who has been waiting to see you. But first, let me give you something for the pain and check the wound." The Wise Woman helped Sol onto her stomach so she could remove the bandages and inspect the wound. A cool, soothing balm carried away some of the anguish her injury had caused, and she felt somewhat better.

Once the Wise Woman was done, she stood and opened the door to reveal Eduardo, his eyebrows drawn together in concern. He glanced between her and the Wise Woman as if asking for permission to enter.

The Wise Woman stepped away from the door and waved him inside. "She's ready to see you. And if you're careful, you could take care of something you previously neglected to do."

His face reddened, and his Adam's apple bobbed nervously. He didn't reply, just blinked at her as if not sure what to do.

"Come in, come in. No standing there like that." She tugged on his arm, and he walked into the hut.

Nervousness fluttered in her stomach like butterflies. Why she had any reason to feel that way now, she wasn't quite sure. The Wise Woman's suggestion to consummate her relationship with Eduardo rang through her ears. Maybe she did know why she was nervous. She'd finally have what she'd wanted.

"You sure she's up to something like that?" Eduardo asked. "It's only been a week since she was stabbed."

The Wise Woman smiled and nodded her head. "I am my people's healer, and I have been for many more years than you've been alive." And with that, she slipped through the open door and closed it behind her.

Sol blinked in surprise. He'd doubted their sacred healer and spiritual guide? "If she says I'm fine, then I am, Eduardo."

His gaze met hers from across the small hut, and he frowned as his gaze drifted over her. "Are you okay?" He strode to her and knelt beside the bed. "I was worried."

"I'm feeling better than I did." She pushed from her stomach to her hands and knees but paused at the soreness in her lower back. The Wise Woman's healing cured wounds quicker than was normally possible.

His hand descended on her shoulder then slid lower toward her backside, missing the bandages. "Are you sure you want to do this?"

She nodded. Although this time she wanted more closeness and intimacy between them than before, which had been great except for the end and its aftermath.

"I just want to find a better position." She lowered herself back to the bed and very carefully turned to her back.

"Do you need any help?" He cupped her hip, brushing his thumb over her skin. Her skirt had slid up when she'd moved, but she wasn't worried about adjusting it. From the look in Eduardo's hungry gaze, she didn't think there would be much point in it anyway.

"No... I just..." She paused, not knowing if she should continue with her train of thought. What if she were right? What if he'd changed his mind or hadn't wanted her as much as he'd thought he did?

"You what?" His lips curved down, and he paused in his stroking of her hip.

"Do you still want me? I want you more than anything ever in my life. I don't want you to feel like you have to do—"

His lips covered hers, stealing her words. He slid the hand that had been on her hip to between her knees. It trailed up and up, and her breath caught in her throat as he cupped her mound. A finger slipped between her folds, and he teased the sensitive bud nestled there.

Her breath caught, and she leaned her head back, savoring his touch.

Eduardo's lips pressed along Sol's neck, and she gasped for air at the sensual contact. Her hands slid into his hair and held him there. Although, she knew he could break free whenever he wanted since he was so strong, and yet with her, he could be gentle and tender.

His finger circled and rubbed her clit until she thought her body might explode in desire, but he pulled away, leaving her there, teetering on the edge of pleasure.

She reached for him as he stood, not wanting the distance between them, but she shouldn't have worried. He gave her a mischievous smile and unfastened his jeans. Her gaze followed his movements as he dropped his pants, and she gasped at the sight of his cock so large and ready. Seeing him like that made her want him even more.

He made his way onto the bed, and she spread her legs for him, giving him room, and more importantly, giving him access to her body. He crawled up to her like the dangerous cat he was, and her heartbeat sped up.

She opened her arms for him, welcoming him to her, needing him inside her. Her body thrummed with the urge to shatter in pleasure, and he'd only touched her.

He covered her with his body. She felt his cock press against her entrance and then steadily ease inside of her. His gaze remained steadfast on hers as if waiting for any sign of pain.

Though she wanted to frown at his abundant carefulness, the fact he did care about her tugged at her heart. "I love you," she said, the words slipping out before she could catch them.

Eduardo stopped. A strange expression slid through his eyes, and she wondered if she'd made a big mistake by saying that. He had been wary of relationships, and now she'd probably rushed him. Finally, he moved inside her again. "I didn't think I'd ever say this to another woman, but I love you too." His mouth dipped to her throat, and he nipped her with his teeth here and there.

She circled her arms around his broad chest in a hug and trailed her hands over the hard, muscular expanse. His thrusting picked up speed slowly, but she felt the fine tremor in his muscles as if he were holding on to his beast. The idea of him ravaging her like he had in the forest sent a sharp surge of pleasure between her legs, and she bit her lower lip to keep from crying out.

He cupped her hip, driving himself in a little harder as her body exploded in waves of ecstasy. She opened her mouth, but Eduardo covered her lips, kissing her hard to muffle her screams of pleasure, which only added more delicious fire to the moment.

His shaft jerked inside her, and he held himself still as his hot seed shot inside her. He leaned forward, pressing his head against the bed next to her, but he remained careful and didn't put too much weight on her. "Sol, you're perfect the way you are. I'm sorry for what I put you through before."

She ran her hand over his back, squeezing his backside. His words made her beam with happiness. "It's okay. We're beyond that, I think, especially now. Besides, I know a few things you can do to make up for it." She laughed, and he leaned back to look at her.

He cocked an eyebrow. "Well, I started by taking your recovered belongings to your new hut."

Her eyes widened. He'd done that for her? "I don't know what to say… Thank you."

He gently tugged her lower lip with his teeth. "That'll work. The only question is, how much should I let you rest before I can satiate more of your desire?"

JUNGLE BURN

1

Sabina Rukan knocked on the door to Tiago's hut. He'd been her closest friend for a while, even though her parents had always preferred her to socialize with the other girls in the village. She didn't really care. Growing up as Princess of the Amazons, she couldn't help a slight feeling of entitlement.

The door to his hut opened, and Tiago stood there shirtless with a faded pair of jeans hugging his hips. He smirked at her with a wicked quirk of his lips.

She trailed her gaze over the muscular expanse of his chest. Seeing all his bare skin made her want to nibble on his torso and bask in its warmth. For the past few weeks, her hormones had gone into overdrive.

She'd noticed the werepuma men taking a greater interest in her, which was embarrassing, and yet her parents were still convinced she wasn't ready to become a woman. If they weren't going to trust her, she needed to take matters into her own hands. She'd known just who to come to.

He took her hand and kissed her knuckles. "Sabina, how are you doing?" His nose twitched a little, and his brown eyes darkened, as they tended to do whenever she came around. He wanted her, and she wouldn't mind having him, either.

"I'm doing well enough. I need to talk with you." She held on to his hand, pulling him out of his hut. With her being a weretiger, she had comparable strength to his, but she'd been taught not to use her full strength from a young age. That would only hurt people around her, which she was very careful about.

He didn't look too sure about this, but he shut the door and followed her. "Where are we going? Why aren't we talking in my home? There's more privacy in there than out here."

She stopped, turned to look at him, and sighed. "Not really. You know as well as I do, if someone wanted to listen in on our conversation, all they'd have to do is stand outside your door and concentrate. That's not okay with what I need to talk about."

At just that moment, a couple of male werepumas walked by them and looked her up and down. One halted his progress, his eyes flashing upon her as if he wanted nothing better than to push her to the ground and ride her. Her out-of-control hormones were a primary cause for the sudden surge of crudeness she faced, yet her Amazon kin wouldn't understand.

Sabina was different from them. She was the only female werecat in the village, and in many ways, it felt like she'd been cursed. Her parents had forbidden the werepumas to tell her secret, and Kyle—their leader—made sure his people knew the lengths he'd go to help make sure the Amazons didn't find out before they were ready. They weren't sure the Amazons would stand behind her as they did her mother, the queen, or even her father or Rubia and Kyle. None of them was a creature next in line for the throne.

Frowning, Tiago shrugged. "Fine. Take me wherever you think is safe."

She walked with him through the village, her gaze set straight on where she was going. Her shoulders were tense, but Tiago used his free hand to squeeze one of them slightly. "Relax," he said.

Sabina let out a breath and took him into the trees. They didn't go far, just enough to have some privacy. "Okay. I..." She paused, not knowing how to go about this. Her usual carefree personality stumbled with letting this off her chest. How could she ask him about her needs? "I was wondering..." She shook her head. "I'm sorry for bothering—"

Tiago hooked his index finger under her chin and forced her to look at him. "You're not bothering me. Just let me know what's on your mind." He stared into her eyes, his gaze intense even in the dark night.

"I need sexual release." The words left her lips before she could cage them. "I hear the mated women and men in their huts, and my body burns like it's caught in a bonfire." She licked her suddenly dry lips, and his gaze dropped to take in the swift motion.

"And you've come to me with this request?" His tone was carefully neutral, but the bulge at the front of his jeans spoke louder than his words.

She nodded.

"Your parents would kill me—hell, my parents would probably help—if I claimed you without their permission." The wicked quirk of his lips teased her. She wanted to punch him in the face, but that wouldn't help her cause.

"And?" She propped her hands on her hips.

"I might be able to help ease your desire." He helped her to the ground then settled her onto her back. His hands went to the strip of cloth covering her chest, and he shoved it down, freeing her breasts. He leaned in, his mouth sucking on her nipple as his hand rolled her other nipple between his fingertips.

The sensation of him toying with her breasts nearly made her cry out, but they weren't far enough from the village for her to do that. If anyone found them, they would both be in big trouble.

Tiago pressed his jeans-clad hips between her legs, grinding his hard cock against her. She bit her lower lip and whimpered. Her response only seemed to embolden him, and he slid his lips down her torso toward her waist. He nipped the skin near her belly, and he gripped her thighs, spreading them open for him. Leaning back, he pushed up her skirt, baring her pussy to the warm night air.

There was no going back now.

Something within him seemed to change, and he'd suddenly become more than the friend she'd had since she was a kid. The intensity in his gaze as he looked her over startled her. Who was this man? Her body tightened, and she lifted her hips as desire rode her.

He took that for the invitation it was. He lay between her legs, shoving her thighs farther apart.

Her breath caught in her throat as his lips teased her moist folds. He parted them with his fingers and trailed his thumb along her slit, but he didn't slide it inside her. She knew he was being as cautious as he could be with her, especially considering the improperness of the current situation. She gasped as his tongue teased her opening before gliding up to her clit.

His fingers tightened on her thighs, and she licked her lips. The idea of a man being able to please a woman like this had never entered her mind. While she wasn't as naïve as some of the young women in the tribe, she was the first to admit to not knowing nearly enough about sex as she wanted.

Desire pulsed through Sabina's body with each stroke of Tiago's tongue over her clit. The tip of his finger nudged her entrance, but he didn't penetrate her. She arched her back and caught sight of the man she really wanted, Rafael.

Damn it! What is he doing here?

He met her stare without flinching. Leaning casually against a tree, he adjusted the front of his pants, not bothering to hide his evident arousal. Did he really think of her like that? Was he just finding pleasure by spying on them?

The distraction caused her to falter, and Tiago nipped her clit with his teeth, causing her to cry out. She brought her hands up to her breasts. If Rafael wanted to watch, she'd give him a good show.

She tweaked her nipples with her fingertips as Tiago had done, and she moaned, pleasure building within her, exciting her to the point of no return. Knowing Rafael was watching fanned the flames of passion building within her.

Tiago's lips closed around her clit, and he sucked hard, sending her flailing into release. A loud cry ripped from her throat. She tried to shut her thighs at the intense sensations radiating from her pussy, but Tiago held her legs open, licking and sucking faster and harder.

She fisted her hands into his shoulder-length blond hair. He growled low in his throat, and before she could react, she was face down on the ground with her ass in the air. Her reaction times were obviously sluggish.

Sabina looked up as movement caught her attention. An Amazon guard patrolled farther off, but she slunk in their direction, holding her spear up, ready to attack at a moment's notice. Rafael must've noticed her too. He held his gaze on the guard for a few moments before staring back at Sabina. His eyes narrowed over her shoulder at Tiago, and she looked back at Tiago to see him watching Rafael.

Suddenly she felt very vulnerable. How were they going to react to each other? There had been cases of male werepumas who fought and died over potential mates before. The last thing she wanted was for that to happen between Tiago and Rafael.

Instead of coming at them, Rafael adjusted his thick bulge again, then headed toward the Amazon guard. The guard startled at his seemingly unexpected appearance before settling down.

"Ah, it's only you," the Amazon said, her voice still sounding a little breathy. "I didn't know. I thought I heard something."

Rafael shrugged his broad shoulders. "Sorry. Just decided to take a walk." His voice held an edge to it that Sabina wasn't sure she liked.

She pulled her top into place and began to slide her skirt down, but Tiago grabbed her hips, keeping her from doing so. He lifted her so she was on her knees with her back rested against his chest. His hard cock strained at the front of his jeans, pressing into her lower back

"I need to be inside you." His voice was strained, and if she hadn't known who was behind her, she would have been scared. He sounded nothing like the man she'd known since childhood.

"We can't," Sabina whispered, closing her eyes.

He leaned his forehead against her head and breathed deep. "I know. Damn..." He pulled back abruptly and fixed her skirt.

She snapped her eyes open, smelling the musky scent of Rafael. He stood mere feet away from them now.

"What's going on here? Tiago?" Rafael crossed his arms over his chest. The two men had been friends since childhood as well. Yet Rafael had always distanced himself from her. With the way his reserved father, the werepumas' second-in-command, was, she didn't have a hard time seeing why he might be so closed off from her.

Sabina pushed away from Tiago, no longer worried about holding back her strength. He reached for her, but she moved away from him, out of his grasp. Her skirt was still crooked, so she kept her gaze away from Rafael and adjusted it, then plucked stray leaves from her hair. It wouldn't do to go back into the village looking like a mess. Her kin would be curious, and she might accidentally give away what she'd been doing.

"Sabina, wait." Tiago stayed on his knees.

Her gaze slid to him. What if he told? She shouldn't worry since he would be in worse trouble than she would, at least eventually. Chancing a glance at Rafael, she saw him staring at her, his gaze intense and following her every move. His nostrils flared, and from the stiff way he held himself, she knew he scented her arousal. Just him being this close made her want to throw herself down and have him do the same as what Tiago had done to her, if not more.

Sabina had to go; she couldn't be here like this. Without further thought, she raced back to her hut.

* * *

When Sabina was out of sight, Rafael turned his attention back to his best friend. Tiago kept his fists balled at his sides, and his gaze remained fixed on where Sabina had gone. Tiago's breath came out in harsh pants, and his cock bulged against his jeans.

Jealousy whipped through Rafael, and he wanted to snarl his displeasure. He'd been watching Sabina ever since they were kids. Unlike Tiago, he wasn't very good with social interaction, and Sabina always seemed to shy away from him, but he caught her stares.

His thoughts drifted back to her orgasm. She'd known he was watching, and yet she'd toyed with her breasts and moaned as if she was doing it for him.

"Tiago, what happened here?" He kept his voice low, not wanting anyone to hear them. "Sabina's parents haven't approved her to become a woman yet. I doubt they'd enjoy hearing about you—"

His gaze snapped to Rafael's. "No! You can't tell."

"What—"

"She came to me asking for release. She's different than the human women. You've seen how the other werepumas react around her. She's in heat. I had to help her."

"You wanted to help her." Rafael's knuckles ached from squeezing his hands into such tight fists. The fact that his best friend had tasted Sabina should've deeply angered him, but he could push that aside since he desperately wanted to taste her, as well.

Tiago ran his hands through his hair. "Fine, maybe I did, but if you tell anyone... My parents would not be happy."

"I won't, but only on one condition..." He crossed his arms over his chest. Should he even be asking this? The idea was crazy, and yet if it worked...

"Sure, what's the condition?" Tiago breathed out a sigh as if he were out of harm's way now.

"I want to enjoy her body too. Next time she needs release, you'll come to me, and we'll both be involved."

Tiago cocked an eyebrow at him as if he were crazy. When Rafael didn't say anything more, his face filled with surprise. "You're serious? Uh, sure... I just never knew you were interested in her. You always seem so distant when she's around."

Rafael rubbed at the building tension in the back of his neck. His upbringing hadn't helped with his ability to communicate his feelings. Besides, how was he supposed to compete with the more outgoing Tiago for her attention?

"Don't worry about it, Rafael. I'm not entirely sure she'll ask again after all this. She looked pretty freaked out. If what you're planning is to happen, we'll need to be proactive."

Proactive? He wasn't the type to be proactive when it came to her. Yet his cock hardened at the possibility of tasting her sweet arousal. "What do you have in mind?"

Tiago's grin lit up his entire face. The look caused a sting of jealousy to flare within Rafael's chest, but he stamped it down. Sabina had gone to his friend, not to him. What if she had her sights set on Tiago to mate with?

He didn't think so. The look in her eyes when she'd caught him watching them, and the way she'd toyed with her body just for him, proved otherwise. He couldn't believe she'd just screw with him out of cruelty. There had to be some attraction or else she wouldn't have given him a show.

"We'll go to her. I even know a spot farther off from the village where we will be able to have some privacy." Tiago jumped to his feet in an elegant, cat-like move. He sauntered the few steps toward Rafael, then clapped him on the back with some force. "This'll be great. Good idea." He laughed and headed back toward the village.

Rafael stood there, wondering if it he'd made a mistake. Had he ruined his chances at being with Sabina? Not been quick enough to show his interest? Time would tell.

Somehow, he'd lost control of the situation. He'd given Tiago the condition to hold something over him, yet now he felt like he was the one with something binding him. They'd see how long that lasted. He'd win this game.

He followed after Tiago, and they went their separate ways to their huts. Tiago lived near his parents and the Amazon royalty. He lived amongst the rest of the people, not too far away, but far enough that he wasn't as close to Sabina as he'd like.

He kept his gaze straight in front of him, ignoring the people around him and trying to dull the raging hard-on that ached within his pants. A few of the women looked his way, even an older woman who was already mated to another werepuma. Her gaze followed his every step, making the hair stand on end at the back of his neck.

He pushed open the door to his hut, then closed it behind him. His balls ached with the need for release. Damn it. If he hadn't followed Sabina and Tiago, he'd never have been put in this crazy situation.

He stripped off his pants, fisted his hand over his cock and tilted his head back at the sensation. He slid his fist up and down his shaft, slowly at first, then picking up speed. He imagined Sabina kneeling before him, her mouth sucking on his tip while her hand pumped up and down his length. The thought of her looking up at him, wickedness and innocence combined, sent pleasure racing through his cock.

He stroked it harder and faster, then switched to caressing the head of his cock. An orgasm tightened his abs, pleasure intensified through his tip and shaft, and he groaned as white, ropy strands of semen shot from him.

When Tiago had been with Sabina, only Sabina had been pleasured, which he was happy about, but would he be able to keep himself under control while she squirmed beneath his tongue? He'd seen Tiago's control nearly shatter earlier. Who said he would be able to stop himself from going too far?

2

Nightmares plagued Sabina's sleep. She dreamt of being kicked out of the tribe and forced to fend for herself. She would rather die than have that happen. While she knew she could survive, she wouldn't want to be alone.

Maybe her dreams were trying to tell her to stay away from Tiago and Rafael, but what if they told what had happened? What if Rafael felt compelled to get her in trouble with her parents? She had no reason to think that, but she didn't know how to take him.

And that scared her.

She stared up at the thatched ceiling of her hut. Sleepiness weighed on her, yet fear pounded through her chest. If she didn't talk with Tiago and Rafael about what had happened, she'd go crazy. There would be time for that later in the evening after she trained with her mother's second-in-command, Sandi.

Sandi's daughter, Telma, trained with Sabina. Telma would be taking over Sandi's position as the queen's second once her training finished. Though Sabina wasn't crazy about Telma, she had the tribe's best interest at heart.

Loud pounding on her door startled Sabina upright in her bed. She looked at the small window to see the first rays of light. Oh, geez... She had an idea who that might be.

The banging continued, and Sabina answered the door to find Sandi and Telma standing outside her hut.

"You know I don't enjoy chasing you down for your training. What would your mother think? Even though she was a wild child like you, at least she arrived for her training on a semi-regular basis." Sandi looked her over, grimacing at what she saw. "Get some clothes on."

Sabina opened her mouth to say something, but the words froze on her lips as Rafael passed by her hut. He was heading in the direction of Tiago's, but he stopped when he saw her. His gaze drifted over her.

Sandi and Telma turned around to see Rafael. Sandi crowded Sabina, blocking Rafael's line of sight, and shut the door behind them. "It's not a good idea to get men riled up like that." She clasped Sabina's chin in her hand and forced her to meet Sandi's gaze. "You could get hurt. You're a tiger shifter like your father, I know, but that doesn't mean a lot when it comes to numbers. That's the son of the werepumas' second-in-command. While I doubt they would risk upset between our people after the peace we've had, there might be those who aren't so happy with you flaunting your body. It's an invitation your parents aren't ready for you to make."

She parted her lips to protest, but Sandi held up a hand.

"Yes, you're not happy with that. You want to become intimate now because your hormones are raging. It's happened to all of us, but I don't need to be the one to tell you that once you mate, you mate for life. You need to think wisely about who you choose." Sandi grabbed Sabina's skirt and top, pushing them against Sabina's chest. "Get dressed, and I'll meet you near the training area. Make it quick."

Sabina watched Sandi leave. When Sandi opened the door, Rafael was nowhere to be found, and Telma looked at Sabina as if bored. She closed the door, and Sabina plopped down on her bed. She stared at her clothes, still smelling her arousal and Tiago's scent on them.

Sandi's words made her think. She couldn't face Tiago or Rafael again. Not after last night. She needed to let her parents decide when it was time for her to become a woman. They knew what they were doing, and she wouldn't risk their wrath. Not when such a big decision rested upon her shoulders. She'd yearned for Rafael ever since she was young, but Tiago had seemed like the obvious choice. They got along well together, he seemed interested in her, and there was a little bit of excitement when she was with him.

However, if Rafael felt the same way about her as she felt about him—not that she suspected that to be the case—she could very well give in to her true feelings. But that would have to wait until her parents saw fit for her to find a mate.

Tossing the clothes aside, she found her other outfit. She wouldn't go around smelling of Tiago and her own arousal. That might make people think the wrong thing. With her father being so close, she'd play things safe.

* * *

After a long day of training, Sabina headed back to her hut feeling exhausted. It seemed like Sandi had worked her extra hard today. Not even the fact that she was a weretiger helped. Sandi had kept pushing until she'd seen Sabina begin to fatigue.

A hand descended on her shoulder, and she glanced back to see Sandi's daughter. Telma shrugged a shoulder. "She only kept on you to help you."

Sabina nodded, not sure what to say. It wasn't like Telma willingly talked to her often. "Yes, I figured that was the case. Thanks."

Telma nodded and began to walk away. "Hopefully, through hard work, you'll gain the maturity to become queen."

Go figure. There had to have been a jab somewhere. Just like Telma to be so infuriating.

Shaking her head, Sabina continued her trudge toward her cabin. She didn't want to deal with anyone else today, and hey, at least she didn't feel the least bit horny. Pushing open the door to her hut, she froze. At her table sat Tiago and Rafael.

Their gazes hit her almost physically. She clutched the door, standing there not knowing what to do. Should she make them leave? She'd thought about confronting them about last night, and yet now, when she was so exhausted, she just wanted to sink into her bed and close her eyes.

"What are you two doing here?" she asked.

"Are you going to close the door, Sabina?" Tiago smiled and waved her over to them.

She didn't move.

"What's wrong?" He slowly stood.

Her gaze flicked to Rafael, but before she could react, Tiago had his arms around her. Rafael closed the door. His body heat warmed her back at his closeness. Sandi had warned her about the werepumas. Surely they weren't out to hurt her, but why were they doing this?

She bucked against Tiago's chest, and her back brushed against Rafael's firm chest. She increased her struggle and Rafael's hands caressed her hips. She paused for a moment, glancing over her shoulder at him.

His gaze stared down into hers. "Don't be afraid. We're not going to hurt you." He bent his face closer to hers.

Her lips parted in invitation. "How do I know that, when you two are restraining me? Should I scream for the guards?"

"That would be a mistake." Rafael slid his hands up her sides.

Her body ignited from that simple caress, and she ground her backside against his hips.

Tiago slid his tongue up her neck toward her earlobe. When he reached it, he bit her softly.

Her pussy clenched, and desire flared between her legs, making her want them both so badly. This wasn't safe. What if her parents or someone else came by?

She renewed her struggling, but it proved useless. Instead, she closed her eyes, concentrating on shifting her body from human to tiger form.

Their grip on her slipped as she changed shape. The snapping and breaking of bones and tearing of muscles forced a hoarse, coughing roar from her shifting throat. Her body reconstructed itself as a tiger.

When the change ended, she stretched and paced through her now incredibly small hut. It always seemed bigger when she was in her human form. She hopped into her bed and lay there with her chin resting on her paws. She closely watched the men, and they stared at her, apparently not expecting this kind of reaction from her.

"Why did you have to shift?" Tiago said, crossing his arms over his chest. He looked a little concerned, but somehow she doubted the concern was pointed in her direction. Maybe that was her exhaustion talking. His gaze flicked to Rafael and back to her. No, Rafael had definitely put him up to something. She just wasn't sure what that was.

She hissed in response.

* * *

Rafael had thought Sabina might be a little skittish about what Tiago had planned, but he certainly hadn't expected her to shift into her weretiger form. Any chance of them talking to her about their intentions and getting a proper response was gone.

He rubbed the back of his neck, trying to ease the tension. Ever since last night, he'd felt like he had a capybara sitting on his shoulders. He didn't like that feeling. Maybe he'd been wrong to put Tiago in charge of them becoming intimate with Sabina. He'd just assumed Tiago would know her better and act in a way that would get them what they wanted.

What the hell... maybe it was his turn.

He took a step toward her, and the claws on her huge paws flexed, digging into her bed. He stopped, not risking the chance that she might strike out at him. He raised his hands in the air. "If you want us to leave, nod. I'd like to talk—"

She nodded before he could finish his sentence.

His lips tightened, and he blew out a breath. "If you change your mind, you know where to find me." He stood and headed toward the door.

Tiago's eyebrows pushed together, and he wore a frown. "Wha—?"

Rafael swung open the door and then shoved him outside. When he'd shut the door behind him, he clenched his hands into fists ready to hit someone. "Next time, we're going to follow my plan," he said, his voice nearly a whisper.

"But you barely know her. I thought that's why you had me come up with something."

"I figured you might come up with something worthwhile instead of an idea that would have her shapeshifting." He walked toward his hut, but

Tiago followed on his heels.

"I didn't know she'd do that. I thought it was a good plan. I've never been in this kind of situation before. How was I supposed to know?"

Rafael couldn't blame him. At least not too much. Neither of them was in familiar territory. "You made your point. I'll try to think of something."

Talking behind them turned his attention back toward Sabina's hut. Adara the Amazon Queen and her companion Rei spoke in hushed tones as they stood in front of Sabina's door. Rafael turned toward Tiago but focused on Adara and Rei's conversation. Tiago seemed to be listening in too.

"She's developing into a woman. You might not want her to, but I smell the difference. If she's not allowed to select a mate soon, she might go against your wishes," Rei said. He held Adara gently by the shoulders.

"I know, but there's—" She let out a breath. "I don't know. Maybe I'm just making excuses. She's grown up so fast. I never imagined the pressure I put my mother under when I was younger."

Adara knocked on the door to Sabina's hut, and even from the distance, he heard Sabina's roar.

A smirk slid across Tiago's lips, mirroring his own. She might've thought they were back.

Adara and Rei opened the door and hurried inside. A startled growl escaped the hut before the door slammed shut again.

"That's good news for us. Maybe she'll feel less inhibited," Tiago said.

Rafael nodded, but he knew the rules of mating. Once she found her mate, she'd be bound with that person for life. Their rules hadn't stated the ability to mate with more than one person. Not only would he be trying to win her affection, but he'd have to win out over his best friend.

"I'll get with you tomorrow about what we'll do." Rafael slapped Tiago on the back, nearly making him stumble as Tiago had done to him the previous night. Then he continued on to his home.

Sabina would be his. He'd wanted her for a long time, and he'd have her.

Yet the more he thought about his plan, the less confident he felt.

None of the ideas Rafael had regarding the ménage with Sabina seemed the least bit feasible. Tiago hadn't been able to figure her out, so what made Rafael think he'd have any better success?

He slumped onto a chair at the short table in his hut, then rested his forehead on the solid wood. Perhaps he was kidding himself. She could tell her parents what had happened in her hut. They wouldn't be happy with Rafael or Tiago.

Their behavior had gone far beyond appropriate. They shouldn't have put their hands on her like that while she struggled against them, and yet he wanted to do much worse than have his hands on her warm skin.

3

Sabina walked home from training the next day feeling even more beat up than the previous day. It was almost as if Sandi had it out for her. Then again, maybe she'd heard about what had happened with her parents.

Sabina couldn't believe she'd roared at them. She'd wanted to be left alone, and she'd suspected it would be Tiago and Rafael back for more trouble. She hadn't paid close enough attention to the source of the voices outside her door. She'd had her paws covering her ears as she tried to relax. That hadn't turned out so well.

Of course, they'd been mostly kind to her, wondering what was wrong. But she hadn't wanted to shift back into her human form. She'd felt so vulnerable and unprepared to talk with them. Eventually they convinced her it would be in her best interest to change back. Of course, then she'd had to spend a while talking to them and convincing them she'd just had a rough day during training.

She wiped away the sweat on her forehead with the back of her hand. If only she'd kept her mouth shut, maybe today wouldn't have been worse. The look Sandi's daughter had given her this morning had been more hostile than apathetic. That had been her first indicator of the day to come.

However, the more she thought about last night and Rafael's desire to talk, the more she wondered if maybe talking to him would be the best for them. He'd get whatever he wanted off his chest, and she would as well. Things would be simpler. And right now simple sounded so good.

She changed directions and headed toward Rafael's home. He lived farther into the village, and she was sure he'd be done with his chores by now. Most of the people in her tribe were. Sandi, however, was like a slave driver. No wonder she didn't spring out of bed to go to training.

Sabina stood before Rafael's door. Part of her wasn't sure this was a good idea. Maybe she shouldn't be here. It could be inviting trouble upon her, but... She shook her head. That was ridiculous. She came to do this, and she would. She wouldn't look like an idiot who ran away from her problems like she had last night.

She lifted her fist and went to knock on Rafael's door, but it flew open. She jumped nearly three feet away, her feline instincts and fluidity propelling her backward.

Rafael stood up straighter. He wore a surprised look on his face. "You're here to talk? Come on in."

A few women behind her whispered about her peculiar behavior. Very few people in the tribe knew she was a weretiger. Her mother worried that if they knew, they might not respect and follow her. However, it was part of who Sabina was, and her feline instincts were hard to control at times.

She hurried inside Rafael's home, preferring not to hear too much of what the women said. Their whispers weren't soft enough for her to miss their speculations, and she hunched her shoulders inward. Maybe she wasn't mature enough to take her place among the Amazonian queens in her lineage.

"Don't you have other things to do aside from gossip about your future queen?" Rafael's voice came out as a snarl that raised the hair on the back of her neck. She hadn't anticipated him standing up for her, especially not in this incredibly menacing manner. The fact that someone would do so meant more than she could've imagined. If only he would take care of Telma, then she'd have it made, but having him growl at her wouldn't give Sabina any power over that relationship; it'd make her continue to look weak and give Rafael an elevated position.

He turned slowly and kept his gaze low as if nervous about her reaction to his outburst. She closed the distance between them and placed her hand on his arm. "Thank you."

Rafael stiffened beneath her touch, and she wondered if she'd done something out of line. She started to pull away, but he placed his hand over hers.

"I'm sorry about last night," she said. "I shouldn't have retreated into my tiger form." Her gaze stayed on his hand, unable to look into his eyes. What would she find there? Then again, neither of them felt very comfortable. That should've made her feel better, but instead, she pondered if coming here had been such a good idea after all.

"It's fine. It was our fault. We shouldn't have cornered you like that." He pulled his hand away and retreated to the table. He held out one of the short chairs and waved her toward it. "Would you like to sit?"

She really looked around his home for the first time. It looked similar to hers, except with less space and a more masculine vibe to it. It felt cozy. She nodded and sat on the chair.

Rafael circled the table to sit across from her. He rested his elbows on the table and let out a breath. "I'm sorry for what we did last night, and even for what I said. You shouldn't have been put in that position. About the other night, I'm sure we can put that behind us. I'd like to—"

A knock at the door interrupted him, and they both glanced toward the entrance.

"Who is it?" he called.

"Tiago. You were supposed to come by so we could discuss your plan for—" Before Tiago could finish his sentence, Rafael was out the door. It slammed shut behind him.

Something wasn't right here. Rafael's plan for what? She strained her ears to listen in on their conversation. She wouldn't be caught unaware anymore.

"What do you think you're doing?" Rafael said. "She's inside. I was talking to her."

Wariness settled into her chest. Part of her wanted to confront them, but she didn't even know if it would be worth the trouble. Aches fatigued her sore muscles, and she should've just gone home. If she had, she wouldn't have put herself into this situation. She would've been blissfully unaware.

"Maybe this is the perfect time to act," Tiago said, excitement raising his voice a little.

An *oomph* and the thud of fist to flesh signaled Rafael had punched Tiago. "Lower your voice, damn it. We don't want her to hear us. I don't think this is the best time. We didn't do the right thing last night, and she looks exhausted from training..."

Sabina frowned and stopped listening. Did she look that bad? Enough of this. She would confront them.

She crossed the room and flung open the door. They turned their surprised gazes on her. "You two should continue that conversation inside where people can't freely hear you, and I'm so sorry that I've had a long, exhausting day." She pushed past Tiago, but Rafael grabbed her by the shoulder.

"That's not what I—"

She turned and shot him a look. "Save your excuses."

He met her gaze with his own, and anger pulsed through his jaw. For a moment, she thought he would let her go, but he tossed her over his shoulder.

Sabina bucked and twisted her body in earnest. The way he clasped her legs tightly to his torso kept her from being able to kick him; besides, if she fully let loose, she'd break his bones, and that wasn't exactly what she wanted, even if he was infuriating her. She slammed her fists into his back, causing a satisfying grunt of pain from him.

Tiago grabbed her hands, and she stared him in the eyes.

"I can't believe you. I thought we were friends," Sabina said.

Pain etched itself in Tiago's face, and he lowered his gaze.

They quickly brought her inside Rafael's hut.

"What are you guys doing?" She lashed out again, trying to get away from Rafael. She managed to shove Tiago off her and into the door, and she pushed away from Rafael's back, at the same time slamming her leg into his stomach.

His grip on her faltered, and she slid off his shoulder. Her body contorted in the air, landing her on her feet. She took a few steps away from them and kept her senses on high alert. She wasn't sure what they were after.

Rafael was hunched over and had his hand pressed against his stomach. He wheezed and watched her, hurt in his eyes.

Tiago remained where he was, but he looked confused and hurt too.

What was going on? Why were both of them behaving like this when she'd been the one who should've been hurt and confused?

"Why are you guys planning in regards to me? I'm not something to just be used for your own entertainment." Sabina backed up a few more steps until her back pressed against the wall. She lightly leaned on it, feeling confused and exhausted.

"We're not plotting against you, Sabina. We've been trying to figure out how to convince you to let us in. We both want to please you." Tiago's words were tight, and she turned her attention in his direction. He truly meant what he said.

"What?" She glanced back at Rafael. He wanted her? Her heart raced in her chest. Could it be?

Rafael nodded. "Yes, it's true. We weren't trying to attack you last night. We unsuccessfully were trying to get closer to you."

She sat at the table before her legs could give out under her. She should've realized that. How could she have been so blind? The way Rafael had run his hands over her skin... she shivered in remembrance.

"You both want me? But my parents... and mating tradition..." Sabina put her head in her hands. "I can't see how that would work."

Rafael placed a hand on her back. Both of them couldn't remain in her life, but they could both give her pleasure before she decided which of them, if either, would be her mate. Although he desperately hoped she chose him.

She stared up at him, but she sighed and looked away.

"We'll give you release. You'll still remain intact for mating." He ran his hand over her back, massaging the stiff tension there. When he glanced at Tiago, he saw jealousy light up in his eyes. He kept going with the massage. While he didn't want to lose his best friend, he wanted Sabina in his life.

"You mean, like the other night?" Her palms muffled her words. She moaned as he hit a knot near her shoulder, then she winced. "Ow!"

"Sorry about that. What has Sandi been making you do?" he asked. When he'd walked by the training area the other day with Tiago and his father, he'd seen Sandi working her beyond normal human capabilities, and while the werepumas knew she wasn't human, no one else should have. Adara and Rei kept Sabina's secret from the Amazon women, since they weren't certain how the people would react to their princess being a weretiger. The Amazons had faced a lot of change, and while they had done well with most of it, that change might be too much for them.

"Way too much. She's like a slave driver these days." Under her breath, she added, "I don't know what her problem is."

Tiago padded across the hut to sit at her side. He placed his hand on hers. "Do you want me to talk to my parents? They could mention something to yours."

She tilted her head to the side, and Rafael could see a bruise on her face he hadn't noticed before. "No, it wouldn't make a difference. Besides, her daughter will be worse." She sighed, shaking her head. "I don't want any trouble."

Tiago glanced his way, and the jealousy was gone, replaced by a slight sadness at Tiago's hurt. Tiago returned his gaze to Sabina. "Are you sure?"

"Positive. Thank you. Besides, if I did say something, it would be better for me to speak directly with my parents. They already suspect something is wrong with me, so if I don't talk to them, and they suddenly find out from your parents that I'm not happy with my training, then I'll have to hear about it from them." She leaned her head against Tiago's shoulder and placed a hand on Rafael's leg, running her hand over his jeans.

The feel of her touch soothed the beast within him. He relaxed a little and let out a breath he hadn't realized he was holding.

She raised her hand higher upon his leg, and she looked at Tiago, her lips close to his. "I doubt this would be a good place for you both to have me. Did either of you think that far in advance?"

Tiago grinned and pressed his lips against hers. Their lips locked in an intimate kiss.

Rafael felt like a voyeur. His cock hardened at the sight of her so willing and pliant to Tiago's mouth, and he bent to caress Sabina's neck and shoulders. He slid his hands lower toward her hips.

Tiago pulled back from the kiss, his breath coming out harder. "I know a perfect place. My mother took me there once when I was a cub. If we're going to, we should probably head out tonight once everyone's asleep. We don't want anyone to get suspicious."

"What about the guards?" Sabina asked.

Tiago cocked an eyebrow at her. "They won't be a problem." He laughed. "As many times as we snuck past them as a kid, I'm surprised you even ask."

Her gaze drifted back to Rafael and a blush made her cheeks rosy.

"He's done so as well. We're guys, Sabina. Getting into trouble is in our nature," Tiago said. He placed his hand on her knee, sliding it up between her legs.

Rafael cleared his throat. "Maybe we should continue that later. Right now we might get ourselves more worked up than we can handle."

Sabina swallowed audibly and nodded. "Good idea."

* * *

Later that night, Rafael slipped passed the village's guards, both Amazon and werepuma, with Sabina and Tiago. They shifted into their cat forms and darted through the rainforest. The warm night felt good as he ran.

The spot Tiago had mentioned was farther than any of them had anticipated, but it was beautiful. Beside them was a tributary of the Amazon River. Although they would be pushing it to get back to the village before morning when someone might notice the three of them missing.

He concentrated on his shift back to human form. His change came relatively easily, except for the intense pain of his body snapping and ripping itself apart before reshaping itself again. Tiago's shift took a little longer than his, and Sabina's took about the same time as Rafael's.

She seemed a little more winded than usual. She lay on her back and looked up at the sky. Her knees were up, and he caught a glance between her legs, enjoying the sight of her pussy. He wanted to mount her, but that wasn't what they were here to do. He moved next to her and lay on his side. He placed his hand on her abdomen and drew small circles around her belly button.

She smiled at him and caressed his cheek.

Tiago circled around to Sabina's other side, then he plopped down on the ground next to her. He placed his hand on her breast, squeezing it gently before he bent his mouth toward the nipple.

Rafael moved his palm down Sabina's stomach, slipping his fingers between her legs. The soft patch of fur tickled his palm as he trailed his finger over her, caressing her lips before delving between her folds. He'd never touched a woman before, so he tried to remember the very few tips his father had given him as well as what he'd witnessed Tiago doing before Sabina climaxed. He let her body's reactions to his touch instruct him.

A moan left her lips, and she arched her hips into his hand. She brought her face up closer to his with her lips parted. He leaned into her and kissed her, gently at first and then more passionately as she opened herself to him more. The playful touch of her tongue sliding across his tightened his body, and he licked, sucked, and tasted her mouth like he so wanted to taste her body.

A loud slurp made him crack his eyes open, and he saw Tiago with his mouth hovering over Sabina's nipple. Lust-heavy eyelids watched him, and Tiago licked her nipple in slow, soft strokes while Rafael watched. Even though both wanted her, it seemed they both were way too aroused for much competition at the moment.

Tiago moved closer to her mouth, and he nodded Rafael, who was still stroking her clit in soft circles.

Rafael pulled away from the kiss, and Sabina held the back of his neck, not wanting him to leave. Her lips were moist and swollen, and she looked into his eyes with desire. He smiled down at her and placed a light kiss on her lips.

Tiago tilted her chin toward him, and her hands slid free. She wrapped her arms around Tiago's neck, her lips parted, and he covered her mouth with his.

Rafael turned his attention toward Sabina's pussy. He parted her legs, making enough room for him to kneel. She opened her thighs wide, and his beast rose up within him to claim her. Make her his mate. He took a few deep breaths, pushing down his instincts. How Tiago had been able to withstand the urge, he wasn't sure. He knelt, and his gaze took in all of what she offered. He slid onto his stomach and blew on her slit. He traced his fingertips over her labia again, enjoying the way her body reacted to his as he teased her warm flesh.

A low, sexy moan echoed from her chest as he parted her lips. He teased her opening with his tongue before sliding it all the way up to her clit. She arched her hips, and he held her in place, wanting to taste her and do all he'd desired to do to her.

Rafael glanced up at her to see Tiago caressing her breasts as he continued to make love to her mouth with his tongue. Tiago moved his mouth down a little, caressing her neck and shoulders. He continued until he reached her breasts. He sucked her nipple between his lips and watched Sabina as she stared down at him, and then her gaze went to Rafael.

Moaning, Sabina ran her hand through Rafael's hair, caressing his scalp soothingly. With her other hand, she held onto Tiago, trailing her fingers over his back. "You two are lighting my body on fire like I'd never known possible. So much sensation."

Rafael circled his lips around her clit and sucked on it, causing her to cry out and jerk within his grasp. He struggled to hold her steady as he continued sucking on her and then sliding his tongue over her clit. Her grip tightened a little on his hair, and he flicked his tongue over the little nub more quickly. Her wetness and the scent of her arousal increased, and he felt the tightening of her thighs beneath his hands. She was primed and ready to orgasm.

Tiago slid his mouth up to Sabina's, muffling the scream of her release just in time. He seemed a bit tenser than he'd been when they first arrived here, but from the raging hard-on Rafael had, he could only guess that Tiago faced the same weakened self-restraint.

Rafael lapped at her sweet juices, wishing he could shove his tongue inside her pussy and taste her more fully, but that risked more than any of them cared for. He pulled away once the waves of her orgasm eased, resting his head against her thigh. She stroked his head and continued to make whimpering moans of pleasure.

Tiago withdrew from her lips and sat beside her. His cock jutted from his body, and he gripped it with his fist, sliding his hand up and down its length.

"What are you doing?" Sabina asked.

"After that, I…" Tiago paused, and his voice was shaky when he spoke. "I need release too."

Her gaze slid down to Rafael. "You as well?"

He nodded, his cheek brushing her thigh and causing her to shiver.

"How can I help you both?" Her voice carried more innocence than should've been there. How could he ask her to satisfy his needs when she sounded so pure?

Tiago's and Rafael's gazes met. Rafael knew Tiago wanted her to, but he didn't feel very comfortable asking it of her. He shook his head slightly, but Sabina pushed into a sitting position.

"I wouldn't ask if I didn't mean it."

"We're fine—" Rafael tried to get the words out, but Tiago spoke over him.

"You place your mouth over us, like we've done for you."

She nodded, not looking the least bit intimidated by the idea. He liked that. She scooted a little away from him, and he moved into a sitting position as well. Her gaze drifted over Rafael's shaft then Tiago's and back again.

"I guess I'll just jump in then." She leaned toward Rafael, taking his cock in her hand. She blew out a breath and moved her hand over his shaft, trying to imitate what Tiago had been doing.

Tiago moved closer to them, and she took his shaft as well. He placed his hands around hers and helped her find a rhythm to stroke his cock. His head tilted back a little, and he groaned. "You're doing great."

The feel of her hand on him was amazing. Rafael never had anyone touch him other than himself. She slipped her hand over his shaft in slow, tentative motions, and he did the same as Tiago had, placing his hand over hers, helping guide her as she slid her hand over his length.

Within a few strokes, her confidence seemed to soar, and she leaned over in Rafael's direction. Her hand still worked Tiago. Her warm breath caressed his tip, and he leaned back a little, balling his hands into fists at his sides. Her hot little mouth closed over his cock's head, and he groaned. He unclenched one hand and trailed it over her shoulder to the back of her neck. He cradled her neck with his hand and wanted to tug her farther onto him, but he stopped himself. Barely. He'd let her have control and do what she felt comfortable with. He wouldn't force any of this onto her.

She slid her tongue over his tip and took more of him into her mouth. Her gaze rose to meet his, and he smiled at her.

He caressed her scalp even more as her lips and tongue worked at his cock. If he hadn't taken his pleasure into his own hands the other night, he might've come in her mouth already. Instead, he could enjoy the sensations of her head bobbing on his shaft and the brush of her tongue against his head.

Her hand still pumped Tiago's cock, and then she paused to brush her thumb over Tiago's tip, smearing the pre-cum over him more fully.

Tiago licked his lips, and when he opened his eyes, they were no longer the normal dark brown. Instead, they were golden like the puma's beneath his skin. He moved away from her grip and sat behind her. He pulled her into a kneeling position, and she withdrew from Rafael and watched him as if cautious of his intentions.

Rafael wondered what exactly Tiago was doing. He tensed, ready to tug Sabina out of the way if Tiago tried anything. Once an Amazon mated, only the mate's death would allow her to potentially choose a new mate—if she wanted to have another mate—and he wouldn't want to do that to either of them.

"Just relax, Sabina. I want to please you while you do the same to Rafael." His lustful gaze remained on Sabina's backside, and his voice was thick with desire. He knelt behind her, his mouth covering her wet pussy while he slid his free hand over his shaft.

Sabina moaned and her eyes tightly closed. She swallowed loudly then looked at Rafael before bending her head back to take his cock into her mouth.

He groaned and lifted his hips slightly, prodding his dick a little deeper into her mouth. She moved faster and gripped his shaft with her hand, sliding it up and down his length as she toyed with his tip. His beast rose to the surface, and he felt his lower stomach tighten. The pleasure in his tip built in intensity, and he heard the soft licking and sucking sounds Tiago was making behind Sabina. Those just added to the moment.

She moaned, and the hum of her vocal cords threw him over the edge. His balls tightened, and he groaned as he came inside her hot mouth. Her body shook with her own orgasm, and she lapped at his cock that much more, sucking his tip and licking up every drop.

Tiago's hoarse groans sounded at the same time as hers. Rafael opened his eyes to see that Tiago had moved away from her a little as white strings of cum spurted from his dick.

Sabina stood on shaky legs, and she reclined next to the water.

Rafael moved next to her and intertwined his fingers behind his head. He knew this couldn't be the last time he had intimacy with Sabina.

4

Sabina lay there in between Rafael and Tiago, her breath coming out in pants. She craved more of them. Tiago scented the air, and he closed the distance between them. He pushed her thighs open as Rafael had done earlier and held his cock in his hand. Lust darkened his gaze, and he leaned closer to her.

She placed her foot against his chest to keep him from coming closer, but he shoved it aside.

Rafael dove at him, knocking Tiago to the side. He pinned the other man down and punched him in the face, splitting open his cheek with the blunt force. "What the hell are you doing?"

Tiago punched at Rafael, but he blocked it. He tried again, but Rafael held on to his wrist. The two men struggled, each trying to gain the upper hand.

"You're both on your own," she said, pushing to her feet. She couldn't believe that the most mind-blowing night she'd ever experienced had turned into macho fighting.

Sounds farther into the forest made her pause. They were coming closer with speed. She crouched and looked around them. This place was beautiful, but it was very open to whoever could possibly want to attack them.

A whistling sounded near her head, and she leaned away a little, feeling the sting of a spear scraping her cheek. It thudded into a tree a few feet behind her. She snapped her gaze toward the direction it had flown from. A male Indian warrior stood there with a handful of others at his side.

"Guys!" Sabina gently kicked Rafael on the leg. "We need to go."

"Shit. Go, Sabina. We'll take care of them," Tiago said. He shoved at Rafael's chest. Rafael relented and darted to his feet.

"Run. We'll be fine." Rafael nodded at her. Anger filled his gaze at the interruption.

She sighed. How could she be fine with letting them stay back while she ran away? If she went, they'd all go, but she doubted they would listen. She wasn't a fragile flower to be hidden away while the men fought. She underwent harsher training than they did.

Besides, if they let these Indians live, they could come after her people again. The three of them had already been stupid enough to come so far from their village. They'd heard the tales of what their parents had been through when the Amazons and Indians' relationships had become volatile, especially Rafael's mother.

She crouched and forced her shift back into tiger form. It wasn't a good idea to do so many shifts in so little time because it weakened her, especially after having two mind-blowing orgasms because of Rafael and Tiago.

Her concentration slipped, and her form started reversing to human, but she renewed her thoughts, focusing on the beast beneath her skin, calling it to the surface. Movement around her and yelling snuck in, piquing her curiosity, but she finished the change.

When she did, she felt her paws give way, dumping her to the ground. She tried to push herself to her feet, but she couldn't.

Ahead of Sabina, Rafael grabbed a thrown spear from the air and tossed it back at the Indian, catching him in the chest. Rafael pulled it out of the dead Indian and threw it at the next Indian, but he dodged out of the way.

Tiago fought another one and moved fluidly like the feline he was. He almost seemed to be toying with the Indian. His gaze drifted in Sabina's direction, and he stopped. She saw the Indian take the chance to stab him with a rugged blade to the chest.

She roared, standing shakily. Her body didn't want to move, but she had to defend him. Had to kill the Indian responsible. Her vision turned red, and her beast took over. She jogged toward the Indian and hit him in the chest with her paws, nails out and slashing his chest all the way to his pelvis. He screamed and sliced her with his knife. Blood soaked her fur from the wounds, and she hissed as the pain enraged her beast.

Rafael came up behind them and snapped the Indian's neck. "Protect Tiago. I'll handle the rest of these men." He bounded toward the first warrior she'd seen, using the dagger from the Indian he'd just killed. He moved fast and slashed it across the warrior's throat, but not before the Indian stabbed his abdomen with his own dagger. Rafael grunted in pain.

She crouched beside Tiago, who held his chest with one hand. "Don't worry about me. Go help Rafael," he said. His hand brushed through her fur, and she leaned into his palm.

Rafael finished off the other two Indians. They had seemed frightened and ready to die. He came back to them, kneeling at their side. "How is he doing?" He placed both his hands over Tiago's chest. "We need to get you to the village quickly. The Wise Woman will be able to help."

"My wounds will heal themselves, Rafael. Don't worry about me." Even as Tiago said it, he grimaced in pain and closed his eyes.

Rafael shook his head and lifted Tiago into his arms. "Come on, Sabina."

She rose on still-shaky legs and followed after them, trying to keep up with Rafael's frantic pace.

When they made it back, the village was mostly quiet. A few guards rushed toward them, but when the guards saw who they were, they stopped. One Amazon guard followed them, watching Sabina carefully as they continued to make their way to the Wise Woman.

When they made it to the Wise Woman's small hut, she opened the door before any of them could knock. Her old, weathered hands waved them in. "You three haven't been behaving. You should never have gone that close to the old village." She looked around Rafael's shoulder and nodded at the Amazon guard, who jogged away.

"I didn't realize it was that close, Wise Woman," Tiago said. His tanned skin was paler than Sabina had ever seen it.

"Shush, you shouldn't have snuck out in the middle of the night to be intimate with the princess." The Wise Woman turned her gaze on Sabina, who was still in tiger form. "You shouldn't be in that form in the village. Your parents, or more aptly your mother, have been trying to keep that side of you a secret. While I don't agree with their decision since you're who you were meant to be, you should still honor their wishes."

Rafael grunted as he lowered Tiago to the Wise Woman's sleeping pad. He lost his balance and nearly fell on top of his friend.

Sabina darted to his side, feeling the ache of the spear and knife wounds all over her form. She scraped her feline tongue over his cheek, and he lightly chuckled.

"I'm fine," he said, his voice a little thinner than she'd heard it before. The blood oozing from his wound proved he wasn't okay, but at least she could tell his skin was ever so slowly knitting itself together.

The Wise Woman waved her away. "Move over so I can do my work, and Rafael, please do the same. I will attend to your wounds as soon as I can, but Tiago's wounds are the worst."

Sabina slowly made her way toward the door, but the Wise Woman's loud throat clearing stopped her.

"Child, I didn't tell you to leave. You shouldn't be going out in that form." The Wise Woman froze suddenly, sending a chill through Sabina and causing the fur on her back to spike up from her neck down her back. She clucked her tongue. "You three are going to be in quite a bit of trouble." Her gaze slid to the door before she settled into position next to Tiago, preparing some herbs for his injuries.

Sabina shivered. Dread slid its fingertip along her spine.

* * *

Rafael heard the faint sound of familiar footsteps. The door flung open, and Kyle and his father, Eduardo, stood there, anger pinching their features.

"What's going on here?" Kyle's voice was strong with the need to be obeyed. His gaze switched from Rafael to Sabina to the Wise Woman and finally Tiago. His face softened a little when he saw his son, then anger flooded back stronger than ever.

The Wise Woman kept quiet, and Rafael knew she was leaving the explaining up to them.

"Dad, I can explain," Tiago said, his voice a little weak.

"I'll hear from you later, in private." Kyle's gaze returned to Rafael, and Rafael knew that left him as the one to have to explain everything. With Sabina in her tiger form, she wouldn't be able to speak.

"But I can—" Tiago stopped as Kyle shot him a look.

Eduardo watched Rafael and crossed his arms over his chest.

"We went into the forest to the place where Tiago said he was conceived." Kyle's lips tightened into a white line, but Rafael continued, "We both wanted to please Sabina."

Eduardo's nose twitched. "Seems like you did so, and yourselves. Is she still intact?"

"Ye-"

The door jerked open again. This time, Rei and Adara stood in the doorway. Rei looked like he could kill someone. His gaze zeroed in on Rafael, then briefly flitted to Tiago and back to him. "You two were intimate with my daughter?" He pushed toward Rafael, but Kyle and Eduardo each held one of his arms, restraining him. "Sabina, what do you have to say for yourself?" He looked over at her finally, and his face flinched.

Rafael looked to see Sabina staring straight at the floor, unable to meet her father's eyes. Her fur was matted with blood here and there, and he could see why her father would be so upset with them. She looked absolutely miserable.

Rafael moved toward her, but he stopped when Rei struggled against Kyle and his father.

"Don't you dare go near my daughter," Rei said. He let loose a pissed-off growl.

Adara placed her hand on his shoulder. "I think you should step outside, my love. I'll talk with him."

Rei took in a few deep breaths and seemed to visibly relax. "No, I'll stay here."

"You're taking up my concentration and space in my home." The Wise Woman cast them a look. "Please take this outside. Sabina can stay."

Sabina made an irritated noise in her feline throat. She crossed the area from where she'd lodged herself near the back of the hut to sit next to Rafael. She nudged his hand with her muzzle. She obviously didn't want him to go, but what could he do? He had to go talk to all of them or else they'd be angrier with him than they already were.

He petted her head, then started toward the door, but she grabbed his hand between her teeth. She didn't bite hard, but the look in her golden eyes was determined. Her teeth sank a little deeper, and he frowned at her. His side ached horribly, and he'd rather do anything but go and have this discussion with her parents and the werepuma leadership. "Let go, Sabina. I'll be back."

"Sabina," Adara said. Her tone was firm but kind.

Sabina released him and hung her head.

Rafael followed the rest of them outside. His father kept his distance, but he watched Rafael. He couldn't tell what his father was thinking. Eduardo wasn't good at showing much in terms of emotions except around his mother. Their love shone brightly.

Adara lead them to his home since it was closest to the Wise Woman's hut. They headed inside. The queen and Kyle sat at his table, but the rest of them stood. Rafael remained standing since his side ached so much he didn't think he'd be able to get back up due to the agony he felt. Hell, this whole discussion at this time seemed a little crazy.

Adara carefully watched him. She kept her features neutral. "You and Tiago were intimate with my daughter?"

How could he answer that? They hadn't penetrated her. But they had tasted her body, and that had certainly been intimate. Rei and the other werepumas would be able to tell if he lied because her scent was on him.

"Yes, but neither of us claimed her as a mate."

Her forehead crinkled, and her eyebrows drew together as if in confusion.

Rafael wished Sabina's parents understood. "She's developing into a woman. As a feline, she has needs—"

"Needs? You two shouldn't have approached her to fulfill her needs." Rei narrowed his eyes at Rafael.

"We didn't approach her. She approached us." That wasn't exactly how it had happened, at least not this time, but he didn't exactly want to go into the longer story, especially the fact that Tiago had been her first choice.

Disbelief widened Adara's eyes for a moment. Rei grimaced, and Kyle and his father kept their faces blank. They seemed like they were trying to blend into the background while Rafael worked to dig himself out of the hole he was in. But a tiny hint of disapproval glimmered in his father's eyes.

"She approached you?" Adara finally said. "She would agree with that statement?"

Rafael nodded. At least he assumed she would.

"I'd been afraid of this. We've waited too long to let her become a woman. You were right, Rei." She turned her head and looked up at her mate. Rei met her gaze and brushed his thumb over her cheek. "She's apparently more than ready."

Rei nodded, but he didn't look at Rafael. He kept his gaze on Adara. "But she can't have two mates. That's unheard of for your people. They wouldn't accept her."

"Yes, she'd have to choose." Her gaze shifted to Rafael when she said that. "Once she shifts back into her human form, we'll let her decide."

The door to his hut opened behind him, and he glanced toward it. The tension in the room ratcheted up a notch, but he let out a breath when Sabina walked in. "I've already chosen," she said.

His chest tightened, and he felt like he might be sick. He steadied himself against the wall of his hut, trying not to be too noticeable about it, but he could tell Sabina had caught his reaction.

"Who have you chosen, my dear?" Adara said, waving her over to the table.

Sabina placed her hand on Rafael's arm and leaned her head against his shoulder. "I've desired Rafael for a while. I choose him."

He couldn't believe his ears. She'd desired him for a while. How had he not recognized her desire? His thoughts turned back to when he caught Tiago and her. She watched him as if giving him a private show. He knew then she meant what she said.

He pulled her in for a kiss. Her body pressed against his, and he bit back a groan of pain at the contact with his stomach. Instead, he swept his tongue between her lips, drinking in her sweet taste.

She pulled away from him and looked down at their bodies. Blood coated her skin, and she looked down at his still-bleeding stomach. "You should get back to the Wise Woman's. She needs to take care of your wound."

He pressed a kiss to her forehead. "I'll be fine. Just needs washed and bandaged." He also needed some pants. Standing there naked didn't tend to bother him; all of them were werecats aside from Adara, and she'd been around them for a long time. Yet he did want to see how Tiago was doing. His friend was probably stressing about what was going on, and Rafael didn't want Tiago to feel more anxiety than necessary.

"Rafael, just let her treat your wound." Her concern caught his attention, and he couldn't deny her.

"Fine. I will. Just for you." Rafael brushed a strand of hair away from

Sabina's face.

Someone cleared their throat, and he turned to see Adara, Rei, Kyle, and Eduardo still there. He'd almost forgotten about them.

"Seems like this conversation is over," Kyle said, piping up for the first time since they'd stepped into Rafael's home. He pushed to his feet and then walked toward the door, passing Sabina and Rafael, who he clapped on the back. "I don't think I have to tell you to treat her well." He chuckled and glanced over his shoulder at Rei.

Rei nodded. "If you don't—"

"Father, I can take care of myself," Sabina said.

His father smiled. "I'm sure you can. Take care. I'll see you at the feast to celebrate your mating." He followed Kyle out the door.

"We'll see you there as well," Adara said. She grabbed Rei's hand, then walked out the door.

Rafael started toward his clothing chest, but Sabina touched his arm. Now that they were alone with the knowledge that she wanted him, he wasn't exactly sure how to react. They had been free and wild out near the river earlier, but this was different. This wasn't just lust.

He opened his mouth to say something, but he wasn't even sure what words he wanted to say. Instead he asked, "Why me?"

Sabina let her hand drop. "Well, I guess I've just wanted you for a long time. You always seemed too elusive, though. Besides, Tiago is my friend. I couldn't necessarily imagine spending the rest of my life with him like that."

"You were standoffish too. Until recently, that is." He brushed his knuckles across her cheek.

She smiled at him. "Come on. Get your pants on and let's make sure the Wise Woman takes care of you." She snuck around him then pulled out a pair of loose-fitting sweatpants for him.

Happiness filled his chest, and he was thrilled that Sabina would finally become his mate. The need to heal so he could claim her made him all that much more agreeable to her demands to see the Wise Woman. He just hoped Tiago wouldn't take the news poorly.

5

Sabina and Rafael walked into the Wise Woman's home to find Kyle already there, kneeling at Tiago's side. Tiago looked upset, but when he saw them, his expression turned neutral. It seemed Kyle had already told him the news.

Sabina hated that she couldn't have been the one to explain since he was her good friend, and she did care a lot for him. She didn't want to hurt him, but her true feelings were for Rafael.

The Wise Woman waved Rafael over to her, and he walked to her to get his wounds treated. He cast a glance back at Sabina and smiled encouragingly.

"Hi," Sabina said. She walked a few steps closer, but she didn't want Tiago to feel even more uncomfortable than he probably already did. "I'm sure your father already told you. I'm sorry. I wish I could've explained it to you myself. I—"

Tiago held out a hand to her. "Don't worry about it. There's no need for apologies."

Kyle stepped away from the bed. "I'll see you all later." With that, he left.

"I'm glad you wanted to tell me," Tiago said. "I probably have taken things too far over the past few days. I don't really blame you for not choosing me."

Sabina knelt at Tiago's side. "It's not necessarily your behavior over the last few days. You're my closest friend, and I highly value that." She leaned her face into his hand. "I've just had to come to realize that Rafael has held my desire for a long time. I never knew he felt the way he does for me."

The Wise Woman laughed warmly as she finished bandaging Rafael's abdomen. "He's Eduardo's son, my dear. You should've seen his mother and father's blooming relationship." She shook her head, and a smile

140

curved her lips.

Rafael grimaced and looked a little embarrassed. He turned his head to the side, facing away from them. "My mother has told me a little about their early relationship."

Sabina could only imagine. His parents seemed happy together now, but she knew his father didn't always show much emotion. Sometimes it felt like her parents showed a little too much in contrast. Sometimes she felt like she needed a little space, but her grandmother had told her stories of how her mother had been wild like her. Sabina couldn't imagine that. Her mother was strong and noble and not the wild child she imagined from some of the stories. Hopefully she could follow in those footsteps someday.

Tiago pulled his hand away from Sabina, and she glanced back his way. "I'm glad you value our friendship. May it continue for a long time, and perhaps if Rafael doesn't mind, we could—"

The Wise Woman cleared her throat loudly. "I'll pretend I didn't hear you say that, Tiago. Besides, you'll find your own woman in time. Then you'll be able to have your own mating pleasures while Sabina and Rafael have theirs."

Tiago released a loud sigh. "If you say so, Wise Woman."

The angry look on Rafael's face was priceless. He crossed his arms over his chest. "The Wise Woman is right. Once we're mated, we'll be together as a couple by centuries-old tradition."

"Fine, you're right. No harm in asking." Tiago closed his eyes. "I'm going to rest a while."

Sabina brushed her hand over his cheek, then stood.

Rafael watched her and held out a hand to her once she turned in his direction. "Let's go rest ourselves. It's late."

Sabina stepped outside to see the sun beginning to rise. She bit her lower lip. Any time now, Sandi and her daughter would be arriving on her doorstep demanding her presence for training. After the sensual evening, the fight last night, and her body repairing her wounds as well as her lack of sleep, plus all the emotions this early morning had brought, she didn't think she'd be able to endure the almost torturous training session Sandi no doubt had in store.

At her side, Rafael caressed her cheek. "Is everything okay?" He stared into her eyes, looking her over carefully.

"Maybe we could go to your place?" She didn't want to explain why. The morning didn't need to be more complicated than it already was.

He nodded. But she could tell from his expression that he obviously wanted to know why she'd asked that. But she knew he didn't want to pressure her. That was just the kind of guy he seemed to be.

They headed to his hut, but Sandi had caught sight of her. Her posture changed, and she stormed over to where Sabina and Rafael stood.

Rafael placed a hand on Sabina's arm and stepped in front of her, apparently realizing what was going on. Sabina stepped forward to stand beside him. Rafael frowned at her, but he didn't push her. "What do you want, Sandi?" he said.

Sandi glanced at him, but she turned her gaze to Sabina. "You should've been in training quite a while ago. Who do you think I am, your nanny? I can't always sit around waiting for you to decide when you want to do something." She looked back at Rafael. "Don't you have somewhere else to be?"

He crossed his arms over his chest and put his shoulders back. "Don't talk to either me or her like that. She's had a long night, as have I. I don't think you'd want me telling Queen Adara how hard you've been training her daughter. You are just jealous that your daughter will be merely second in command as you have been."

She stared at him, hostility in her gaze. "You should've listened to me, Sabina. Werepumas aren't trustworthy."

Rafael took a step toward Sandi, but Sabina put a hand on his arm, holding him back, even though part of her wouldn't mind if he did go for her. Right now with their chance at a life ahead of them, she didn't want anything standing in their way.

"I'll be speaking to my mother. Neither you nor your daughter will be pushing me around anymore. I am the princess of the Amazons." Sabina tilted up her chin, trying to feel the confidence and display the kind of aura her mother would if she were in this situation.

Sandi blinked at her as if surprised by her sudden confidence. "Fine, but don't expect anything to change." She stomped away.

Somehow, Sabina doubted that. Things would change because she'd soon be mated with Rafael.

"Don't let her get to you." Rafael rested his hand on Sabina's shoulder, and she leaned her head against him. If only things could be that easy.

* * *

Sabina curled up closer to Rafael and opened her eyes. She didn't know how long they'd slept, but she enjoyed having the warmth of his body against her. She ran her hand over his chest, enjoying his hot skin beneath her fingertips. Trailing her hand lower over his abdomen, she paused just above his belly button.

Rafael's eyes were still closed, and she wondered what he would think if she were to please him now while he was still sleepy. He cracked an eye open. "You're going to stop there?"

She laughed. "I don't know. Should I? I wouldn't want to disturb your rest." The bandages over his abs had some blood staining them, but it wasn't too much. His body was healing quite well.

"I'm fine, Sabina. Don't worry about needing to be careful with me. Besides, I should be the one that's careful with you." He stroked her cheek and then tugged her down beside him. He slid his hand between her thighs until his fingers caressed her slit.

She spread her legs for him, wanting the feel of him inside her, wanting to be mated with him.

He traced his fingers across her folds, but he almost seemed hesitant to do much more to her than that. Just when she was about to say something, he slipped a finger into her, and she gasped at the delicious feeling. She arched her hips against his hand, wanting more.

He smiled and pulled out before sliding his finger back into her. "You're so wet already."

"For you." Her voice came out rough and husky. She could barely recognize it.

The look in his eyes shifted from happy and smiling to something darker and more lustful. He covered her mouth with his own, pressing his tongue between her lips and caressing hers. He nudged her thighs wider apart, making room for him to kneel between her legs.

She could barely contain herself. Her hips ground against him as he pressed against her. She'd tasted him, but now she'd be able to experience what she'd imagined would be the best moment of her life.

The tip of his cock pressed against her entrance, and she took a deep, gasping breath as he entered her slowly, sliding in inch by inch, breaking the wall of her virginity in the process. She bit her lip to keep from crying out. Her body must've tensed, because he stopped moving.

"Are you okay?" he asked, concern in his voice.

She nodded. "I'm okay. Just please, don't stop." She placed her hands on his shoulders, hugging and holding onto him. The feline within her stretched and demanded more from her mate. "Take me. I need you."

He thrust within her again, slow and steady. His large cock filled her pussy so fully, just like it had done with her mouth. She'd enjoyed the taste of him and the experience. She would most definitely have to do that again.

Desire heated her body, and he pressed his hand between them, caressing her clit with his thumb, stoking the fires within her even more. She drew his head down, pressing a kiss against his lips and sliding her tongue into his mouth, caressing his tongue and the inside of his mouth.

His hips picked up speed, and he thrust within her ever faster as if part of him were slowly losing that finely kept control. His strong arms trembled a little in effort.

She dug her nails into his shoulders; pleasure built within her until she knew her body would be thrown beneath the waves of impending orgasm. She clung to him, feeling like he was the only thing real in her world.

He was her rock.

Rafael slowed his pace, but she couldn't have that. She needed more. She shifted their weight, rolling them until she was on top. He stared up at her, surprise widening his eyes. He held onto her thighs as she rolled her hips, taking him even deeper inside her.

She threw her head back and bit her lower lip. She slapped her hand over her mouth, muffling her cries. Her body trembled with pleasure, and finally exploded, sending ecstasy pulsing between her legs.

Beneath her, Rafael's hands tightened on her, holding her upright. His hips thrust up into her. He let out a low groan, and his hot seed filled her pussy.

The only sound echoing through the hut was their labored breathing.

She looked down at him after a moment, and the look on his face was sexy male contentment. His hands moved up her torso to cup her breasts, holding them in his rough palms.

"Once the mating feast is over, we should do that again." He brushed his thumb over her perky nipple, and she moaned at the delicious sensation.

"Yes, we should. My beast will need plenty of satisfaction while she's in heat." She placed her hand over his. "Do you think you'll be up for the challenge?"

Rafael's eyes darkened. "I will. I'm just worried if you'll be able to handle it." He smirked and lightly pinched her nipple.

Sabina rotated her hips, sliding him out and back into her. "Oh, I can handle it. I'm a tigress." She flashed her teeth.

6

Rafael placed his arm around Sabina beside the bonfire. It was lucky he could still walk after their earlier encounter. Thankfully they'd taken a nap, and he'd had a chance to rest before they'd mated and consummated their relationship. She had been a wild tigress. Seeing her above him, sliding his cock in and out of her tight pussy... He'd been in absolute bliss.

Across the feasting area, he spotted Sandi talking to Rei with her daughter hanging back behind her looking nervous.

Rei's features were fierce, but he kept his voice low enough that no one else would be able to hear—not even werecats—unless they were closer.

"You talked with your parents about Sandi's treatment, didn't you?" he asked. He knew she'd left a little while after they'd made love for the third time, but she'd just said she had to change for the mating feast.

"Yes. I'm not going to let her think I'm weak. She should treat me better than she does." Sabina leaned her head against him. "My mother said she'd talk with her, but my father wanted the chance to do so. He said he'd make sure she backed off. There might've been mention of her disgracing her family line. Others of the tribe will be looked at for the second-in-command position."

The punishment was severe, but with the way Sandi's daughter treated Sabina, he could see why the measure might be put into place. She didn't need to deal with that when her time to reign finally came.

Rafael turned his attention away from Rei and Sandi, and he spotted Tiago talking to the Wise Woman's dark-haired granddaughter. Tiago laughed and leaned in closer to her ear. Even beneath her tanned skin, Rafael could see the Amazon blush profusely. Her eyes were wide, and she leaned into Tiago as well.

Tiago pulled away quickly, and he blinked at her. His lips formed a small

145

"o," then his customary smirk curved his lips.

"Looks like Tiago has found someone to keep him company after all," Sabina said.

Rafael hugged her closer to him. "Yes. I'm glad. He deserves to be happy too. Besides, if it wasn't for him, I might not have found my backbone."

Sabina pinched his thigh. "Who knows? Maybe, maybe not. I'm glad we won't have to find out."

He brushed his lips against hers. "No, we won't, and for that, I'm eternally grateful."

AUTHOR'S NOTE

Thank you for reading *The Amazon Chronicles*! These novellas mean so much to me with their strong werecat heroes and equally tough heroines. I was first inspired to write these books after doing research for a paper about the Spanish conquistador Francisco de Orellana and his skirmish with a group of warrior women. While some think the women he encountered might be long-haired male indigenous people, but I couldn't stop thinking about the possibility of a tribe of women living in seclusion in the Amazon Rainforest.

If you enjoyed this book, please consider leaving a review at the retailer's website or even Goodreads. It really means a lot to authors! Also, if you're interested learning more about my books, sign up for my newsletter is available at my website and connect with me on Twitter and Facebook.

www.sarahmakela.com
www.twitter.com/sarahmakela
www.facebook.com/authorsarahmakela

OTHER BOOKS BY SARAH MÄKELÄ

ABOUT THE AUTHOR

Sarah Mäkelä loves her fiction dark, magical, and passionate. She is a paranormal romance author, but she's written all over the romance spectrum with cyberpunk, sci-fi, fantasy, urban fantasy...even a sweet contemporary romance!

A life-long paranormal fan, she still sleeps with a night light. In her spare time, she reads sexy books, watches scary movies (and Ghost Adventures), and plays computer games with her husband. When she gets the chance, she loves traveling the world too.

Find her online at www.sarahmakela.com.

www.ingramcontent.com/pod-product-compliance
Lightning Source LLC
Chambersburg PA
CBHW071258130626
46556CB00003B/1372